INVOLUNTARY LOVE

SHADOW KAI WRITING GROUP   M. R. RICHARDSON
MONICA SHELTON

Acknowledgments

Thank you to everyone I have met along the way who have given me advice and so much useful information. I could not have done this without the support of my convention friends, professional authors, close friends, and family.

Chapter One

Brian closed the program he was working on and pushed back from his desk. Rubbing his hand through his short, dark hair, he looked at his VR googles laying on the desk. Brian glanced at the clock. He was supposed to have met Chad in VR five minutes ago. He could see the blinking alert on his desktop telling him he had new replies on the message boards. His hands hovered over the keyboard wanting to open the messages. Letting out a big sigh, he released the keyboard and picked up his googles. Moving over to his VR couch, he started hooking up the feeds to bring the whole system online. He had recently upgraded. The new system was supposed to make everything "feel more real than real."

"I don't know why I let Chad talk me into this," he commented to himself. He could just about guess what would happen. He would be at a club and all the girls would talk to Chad. It would be as if he were in an invisible bubble. Eventually, Chad would decide to drop back to the real world to hook up and he would be awkwardly left alone with Chad's cast offs. None of whom would want to talk to him. "Why do I do this to myself?"

Brian looked at the information Chad had sent him and groaned. They were supposed to meet up at Nebula. Over the years, many VR clubs had learned from their client's disappointment when they met someone in the real world and they did not match up to their avatar in VR. Patrons would feel scammed, often blaming the club for letting it happen. Some clubs -- realizing the idea of truth in marketing -- had started catering to this. They advertised that their patrons' avatars and their real world personas did not match. Over time, people had gotten wilder and wilder. At those clubs, watching the various avatars was as much the entertainment as any band or show, with people watching as each avatar became more and more alien trying to out-do each other.

Other clubs had gone in another direction, creating strict rules about what enhancements and changes their patrons' avatars could and could not have. As tech improved, they created filters that were able to strip even the smallest enhancement code. The result was your avatar looked exactly like you other than any posted allowed modifications. Of all the club like this, Nebula was the strictest. The only enhancement they allowed was clothing.

Brian looked at his reflection in the computer screen. His round face appeared vaguely moon like in the screen distortion. His short hair hung limply around his face. The last club he and Chad had went to, he had been able to sneak his body slimming code through. It only reduced his weight by about 50 pounds, but that was enough to slim his face and reduce his overall doughy figure. It was never going to make him look as athletic as Chad, but it was something. At Nebula, he would not even be able to use that.

This is going to suck, Brian thought as he reached for his glasses. *This is the very last time I do this.*

The first thing that Brian saw as he entered the program was a giant screen.

ALL MODIFICATION OTHER THAN CLOTHING ARE NOT ALLOWED. A FULL SCAN WILL BE CONDUCTED ON ALL WHO ENTER. THOSE WITH MODS WILL HAVE

THEM STRIPPED. THEY WILL BE SUBJECT TO
PENALTIES UP TO AND POSSIBLY INCLUDING BEING
PERMANENTLY BANNED.

Brian signed at the bottom and hit the accept key. The screen
immediately dissolved and he was in the entry portal. Nebula had
designed their entry to look like an old-fashioned library in a
mansion. All the walls were floor to ceiling bookcases. The
ambiance of the room was so real, you could almost smell the musty
scent of the old leather bindings, glue, and paper of the books. A
hanging wooden ladder was made to circle the room on brass rails,
allowing a person to access any book. A small wingback chair with a
plush footstool sat to one side of the room. By it was a small side
table holding a single curved desk lamp. The light was directed at
the chair for reading. On the other side, an impressive oak desk with
a straight back wooden chair took up most of the area directly in
front of those bookcases. An ornate desk lamp and a computer
screen were the only items on the desk.

Sitting behind the desk was the avatar for the club. "Hello, I'm
James -- your entrance guide. How may I be of service?"

Brian looked at James. He seemed so lifelike. Even knowing he
was an artificial construct, Brian could not find any proof he was
not real. The construct was designed to fit the setting and to be
unassuming to the guest. He was of medium height and build. His
brown hair was cut short, but not too short. His facial features were
pleasant. But he had nothing distinguishing that would make
someone remember him later. Waiting on Brian to answer him, he
stood ramrod straight. If Brian was not deceived, it appeared he
had a slight upward tilt to his nose. Brian knew it could not be true,
but he felt as if James was sneering at him. "I need approved
clothing modifications and entrance to the club."

The entrance keeper tapped on his computer and the room
shifted. Suddenly, a section of bookcases were gone and a door
appeared. "Clothing programming is available through there.
Return here for scanning once you are complete." His current
assistance no longer needed, James sat down.

Brian entered through the door. The room had full mirrors on three of the walls. The fourth wall was made up of a computer keyboard, screens, and a virtual rack of clothes. As Brian began typing his specifications into the computer, the rack of clothes changed to fit his input. Brian tried putting some tailoring specifications into the system that would help hide his weight. The system seemed to accept some, but rejected others as being "outside of normal parameters." Brian sighed and accepted what the machine would give him.

After finding an outfit he like, he pushed a button. The space around his avatar shimmered. Brian always found this part disconcerting, so he shut his eyes. Counting to 10, he opened them. He turned to study his appearance in the mirrors. Brian had selected black jeans because he thought they might be slimming. He had selected a cotton striped pastel t-shirt with a light gray jacket. His hopes were the jacket would hide some of his bulk. Looking in the mirror seemed to confirm his worst thoughts about himself. All he saw was a pudgy 24-year-old trying to look hip and failing. Deciding it would not do any good to try other clothes, he pushed accept and exited back to the entry way.

As he entered, James rose from the desk and walked towards him with a small black wand. "Let me scan you, sir, and then you are clear to enter the club."

Brian stood still as James moved the wand slowly over his form. When the wand reached his hand, it gave a small beep and a light flashed red. Brian looked down and realized that he was "wearing" a ring that was from a previous night out. He quickly made it wink out of existence, glad now that he had not tried to use his slimming mod.

"S-s-s-sorry about th-that," Brian stutter. All he needed was to get banned. He could just hear Chad's voice in head. "What did you do?" On second thought, maybe it would not be so bad. He would have an excuse why he didn't come tonight. Best of all, he would never have to get invited again.

James pushed the reset button and re-scanned his hand. This time the machine had no response. "That is okay. We understand that sometimes small things get overlooked. Just try and be more thorough next time." As he finished speaking, he waved the wand towards the door. It shimmered slightly for a few seconds and then re-solidified. It looked vaguely different, but Brian would be hard pressed to say how.

"Go on through," James stated. Brian let out a breath he had not realized he was holding and grasped the doorknob.

Chapter Two

As soon as Brian stepped through the door, the wave of music hit him. He stood for a moment just inside the door letting his eyes adjust. The club's light setting was at twilight. The dance floor was lit with multi-colored strobe lights flashing above it. Around the edges of the floor, in the gloom outside the lights, were seating arrangements of tables, chairs, and couches broken apart into alcoves to create privacy. Each table had candles giving just enough light for those sitting there to see each other.

Brian began to move cautiously to the right. He went up two steps and moved behind the first row of seating. Up here, people stood at the railing watching those on the dance floor below. More tables and seating arrangements were farther back along the wall. Brian continued to thread his way between those standing and the seating area to get to the back wall and the bar. He hoped Chad would still be there even though he was late. Otherwise, how would he ever find him in this crowd.

Nebula used the best of the real world and VR to creating a nightclub that could never function in the real world, while still striving to seem "real". The back wall of the club was comprised of shelves full of various liquors from all around the world and "the galaxy" as the club like to advertise. The bartenders used what they called an anti-gravity controller to pull the bottle the customer ordered off the shelf and to put it back. It was really just a code of VR being manipulated to move the bottles. Much of the rest of the bar, even the VR constructed bartenders, looked like the real world. They were so realistic you could also forget you were in VR, making the floating bottles appear magical.

Brian moved to the corner of the bar and tried to look down the length of it for Chad. He struggled to see past all the patrons without invading anyone's space. Nebula had the best programmers, so as long as you had a top notch VR set at home, the whole sensation was as if you were there. Brian could hear the music, feel the bass in his bones. He could have actually tasted the beer or liquor if he ordered a drink. It just would not get him drunk or provide his body with nutrients. Brian knew of people that VR became so real to them, that they refused to leave and would die of thirst if someone did not find them and remove their VR gear forcing them out.

Brian was just about to turn around when he felt a hand clap him on the back of the shoulder almost driving him to his knees. *Chad*, he thought turning towards him, *he always has to show off.*

Chad stood to his left with his dimples flashing as he smiled at Brian. He leaned in so that he could speak directly into Brian's ear, "You're late."

Brian looked at Chad and shrugged. "I had to finish a project."

Chad arched an eyebrow and said, "Admit it you almost didn't come."

Brian just stared at Chad unwilling to admit he was right.

Chad broadened his grin and laughed as he ran his hand through his perfectly tousled blond hair. "We are going to have fun," Chad told him clapping him on the back again.

Brian braced himself to keep from staggering. "I don't know. Things never turn out well for me here."

Chad pulled back and looked Brian over. "You really should dress for success more as they say," he replied, as he ran his hands down his outfit. Brian looked at Chad's impeccably tailored suit with just enough flare that it looked more fun than boardroom and then down at his own rather boring ensemble. "I don't know why I even bother," he mumbled to himself.

"What did you say?" Chad asked.

"Nothing," replied Brian, "just that I'm not sure why I did come. I never have any luck with girls."

Chad smiled again. "I know this is kind of fancy for you here, but that's why you have me."

Brian looked at Chad, rolled his eyes, and said, "You really just have me here to pick up your leftovers. Frankly, I was hoping Alison from work was going to be here. I haven't seen her in a while."

Chad looked around the room. "I don't know. Brunette, right? Short, skinny, cute little nose? I don't know if I have seen her."

Brian said, "I was really hoping I would get to see her tonight. I have been wanting to ask her out."

Chad pulled back. "I thought you were here so we could hang and party together. You are just using me to get to girls?"

Brian shook his head. "No, that's not it, at all. Besides, you always end up leaving with some girl. Not me. I'm not sure why you always get to be the one to get the girl."

Chad looked hurt, but then smiled. "I can't help it if I just have the luck, but maybe tonight is your lucky night. Just play it cool and don't be so obsessed. I'm sure we can find you a girl."

"You don't understand. It's not just here. I never have any luck anywhere."

Chad furrowed his brow. "No luck anywhere? I'm not sure what you mean."

Brian attempted to pull away. "Forget I said anything. I want a drink."

Chad put his hand on Brian's arm as if to pull him back, but Brian snapped, "I mean it, just forget I said anything. I am not sure why you care."

Brian turned to the bar and flagged down the bartender. Ordering a whiskey neat, he waited for them to bring it.

After Brian's drink arrived, Chad smiled again and tugged on his arm. "I have seats over here and some people for you to meet."

Brian followed in Chad's wake to one of the seating alcoves. A short table with a glass top was surrounded by two chairs on one side and a low couch on another. Seated on the couch were two of the most flawlessly beautiful women Brian had ever seen. Usually Brian only saw beauty like this created by mods.

The woman on the right was dressed all in black. She wore a sheer shirt with a plunging neckline that showed her black bra. Her black mini skirt was so short, she had to sit very carefully or she would have been flashing whatever color panties she was wearing. Her golden hair was piled on top of her head with carefully placed curls falling down around her face. She had skin that was as smooth as cream. Her icy blue eyes focused on Brian as he walked up.

The woman on the left was dressed in an oversized, bright red men's shirt that she was wearing as a dress by cinching it in at the waist with a large black belt. The bright red was making her olive skin appear almost golden in the club's lighting. Her midnight black hair fell straight past her shoulders and halfway down her back. Brian looked into eyes so dark brown they almost appeared black in the dim haze of the club. She had enhanced the look with makeup making her eyes stand out and her lips were painted bright red with lipstick that had to be custom made to match her clothes so perfectly.

These women are completely out of my league, Brian thought. *Chad says I'm obsessed with women. What about these women. What am I even doing here?*

Chad flopped down on the couch between the two women gesturing for Brian to take one of the chairs across from them. "This is Jolene," he said, as he put his arm around the one on the right. The golden-haired woman gave Brian a slight nod. "This is Cindy," Chad stated, as he put his arm around the olive-skinned beauty to his left. "I told her she could be Cleopatra."

Brian sunk awkwardly down into the overstuffed, low sitting chair. He knew with his weight it would be a struggle to climb out later. He hoped the women would not be there to see his embarrassment. At times like these, he cursed under his breath how realistic the VR experience was. He knew he needed to shed a few pounds, but seriously, couldn't he just catch one break. Oblivious to Brian's problems, Chad went on with introductions. "Ladies, this is my friend, Brian, I was telling you about."

Brian smiled at both women. "Hi. Nice to meet you."

The women smiled at Brian, but did not answer him. Everyone sat there staring at each other. Brian could feel sweat starting to run down his back. But he could not begin to figure out what to say. Chad removed his arms and leaned forward laughing. "I just need a red head and I will have a complete set."

Cindy laughed and pulled Chad back. "You only have two arms, baby. You don't need anyone else."

Chad leaned over and gave her a kiss. "Don't be jealous. You have to play nice. My friend, Brian, here is very lonely. He tells me he has never had any luck with the ladies. We need to find some friends for him to play with."

Brian felt the rush of blood to his face as he flushed as both women turned their gazes on him. Under their stares, he could feel himself sinking down, like a turtle pulling into his shell. But unlike a turtle he had nowhere to hide.

Jolene broke the silence. "Do you mean you have never had a date?"

Brian took a gulp of his drink. The whiskey burned his throat almost choking it closed. Coughing, Brian gasped for breath. "Umm --- can I ----- have----- some water ----- please?" Brian asked between coughs.

Chad snatched a glass of ice water off a passing waitress' tray and handed it to him. "Ladies, please leave us. I need to talk to Brian."

Both women complained, but at Chad's insistence, they rose and moved away a few feet. Enough that in the noise of the club, Chad and Brian could talk alone.

"Brian, have you ever had a date?" Chad asked. "Tell me the complete truth."

Brian tried to stare Chad down and look insulted. But after a few seconds, he crumbled and looked down mumbling. "No."

Chad leaned forward. "I did not hear that."

Brian looked back up and with defiance stated, "No."

Chad stated, "Have you ever had sex with a woman before?"

Brian flushed red again and looked away. Chad was his friend, but this was not really any of his business. He should have just kept his mouth shut. But Chad would not let it go.

"Brian, look at me," Chad commanded. "Have you ever had sex with a woman?"

Brian hung his head and shook it 'no' -- too upset to answer.

Cindy and Jolene drifted back towards Brian and Chad. "We are bored," Cindy purred, as she cuddled up to Chad wrapping herself around him.

Jolene moved to his other side and kissed him deeply. "We don't really want to just sit here and talk."

Chad slowly pulled himself away from the women. "Give me just a few seconds more." He looked at Brian and gave him a shrug as he arched his eyebrow. "I just need five more minutes with my friend here.

Cindy pulled back. "Fine, but if you think I'm hooking up with that in the real world, you have another thing coming," she said, as she flounced away.

Jolene pulled Chad's face to her and used her sensual lips to kiss him deeply. When she was done, she ran a finger around Chad's full lips and stated, "Don't make me wait too long."

Chad turned back to Brian. "Is that why you are always so obsessed with if I went out on a date. If I scored. If I was going out on another date?"

Brian didn't trust his voice, so he just nodded.

"Why you are always talking about women and seem so obsessed with when and where you can meet up with them?"

Brian nodded again.

Chad paused staring at Brian deep in thought. He glanced over at Cindy and Jolene. They were pouting and shifting from one leg to another. Shifting his gaze back to Brian, Chad tapped his lips with his index finger.

"Chad," called one of women. Chad looked back and forth between Brian and the women.

"I have to go right now. But I think I have something special for you. Keep an eye out. I will be sending it to you soon. It's time to hit the real world with one or both of those lovely ladies."

"B-b-b-but-" Brian started.

Chad held up his hand. "I know. We were going to hang. But I thought you weren't coming. You didn't think I was just going to sit here twiddling my thumbs. Next time be on time. Anyway, it doesn't matter," Chad stated as he stood up, "what I'm going to set up for you is even better."

Brian struggled to get up out of his chair. "What am I supposed to do here without you? You can't just leave me."

Chad just shrugged and turned away. "Next time be on time. Maybe find that Alison you are always going on about." Brian got to his feet just as Chad reached the women and put his arm around both. Looking back over his shoulder, Chad smiled showing both dimples. "Be on the lookout."

Chapter Three

Brian turned and watched the dance floor. Down below, he caught sight of Alison from work. He could see her dancing with some other female co-workers. She was smiling and laughing as she twirled on the dance floor. Her dress flared around her, a strategically placed slit almost revealing everything she was or was not wearing underneath until the swirls of fabric from her skirt swung back into place covering it all. She had her chestnut hair down and it streamed around her face matching her skirt as she danced.

During a break in the music, as if sensing his gaze, Alison looked up and spotted Brian. Making eye contact, she immediately smiled at him, her whole face lighting up. She excused herself from her friends and began to make her way towards where he was standing. Brian turned to watch her approach admiring the way her dress continued to swirl around her toned body.

"Hey," she said, as she got close. "I never thought I'd see you here."

Brian just stared at her, drinking in her beauty. He had always thought she was the perfect woman, but tonight she looked extra beautiful. Her hazel eyes seemed to flash green, then brown, then green again in the strobe lights. Her whole outfit had been designed to complement her coloring and to show off her muscle tone. Once again Brian kicked himself for not knowing how to dress better.

"It is nice to see you. I don't know when I saw you last," Brian stated.

Alison smiled. When she smiled, it was if her whole faced lit up. Her eyes seem to be full of fire and her face glowed. "I'm glad I saw you. I was just thinking about you the other day. I realized I had not talked to you in ages. And your friend that we used to hang with all the time. What was his name?"

"Chad," Brian answered.

"Yes, that's it. Chad. I have not seen him in forever either. I'm guessing he is the one that got you to come here tonight. I don't see this being your pick of places for the evening."

Brian shyly nodded. "Yeah, he talked me into coming."

Alison looked around. "I don't see him."

Brian replied, "He already left. I was just getting ready to leave when I saw you. I have to work tomorrow and I'm just ready to go." Brian did not want to explain that Chad had ditched him yet again.

Alison smiled. "I hear ya. Late nights make early mornings suck. You know we really should get together sometime. I miss all you guys that I never get to see any more."

Brian could not believe what he was hearing. Alison missed seeing him. Was she being serious or just polite? How would he be able to know? Brian started to get up the courage to ask her out, when a new song started playing. Alison looked down at her friends on the dance floor. They waved for her to come back down.

"I really have to get back to them. But I am so glad that I got to see you. I hope we bump into each other again soon." With that, she turned and headed back down.

Brian watched her leave as various things he could have said to her floated through his head. He had his chance and now he had blown it. All he had to do was open his mouth and ask her. But, oh no, he had just stood there when she opened the door. Brian decided it was time to leave. He looked for an exit portal and started threading his way through the crowd to the nearest one. He could not believe how horrible the evening had gone. Worse than he would have ever guessed.

Chapter Four

Brian pulled his VR googles off his face and tossed them on the floor. Pushing himself off his couch he stomped to his computer. He knew better than to have gone. But he went anyway. He started to blame himself. Why had he been so stupid?

Once he reached his computer, he logged into the INCEL message board he ran. Starting a new topic, Brian typed frantically as he poured out his experience at the club into the post. He talked about how he had expected it to go poorly and went anyway. He expressed his embarrassment with the women at the club. He vented all of his feelings ranging between self-pity and woman bashing. Frustrated and lonely, he pushed send to post his message.

Brian turned to go get something to drink. Before he had a chance to get up, he heard the familiar ping. Someone had already replied to his message.

"This is not your fault! Those women are the problem!"

Before Brian could even finish reading, the next reply popped up.

"The only thing you should feel at fault for is thinking women could ever be appropriate. They are dumb sluts and stuck up bitches."

Brian typed back, "I just would really like to believe that some-day, I could have a real relationship, but when that fails, I feel like I failed."

The replies started coming faster and faster. Brian could barely keep up with them as he read through them.

"Some women just think they are beneath us. If we aren't Jason Momoa, they aren't going to give us the time of day."

"All these men who get woman after woman, they ruin it for the rest of us. I say one man should have one woman. Make a lottery and you get who you get and you don't throw a fit."

"Some of these women are no better than whores, but they are controlling. They will only be that way if you have looks, money, or power. I say if they are whores, they shouldn't be able to tell anyone 'no'."

One man, screen name TakeTheBlackPill, replied to the last comment, "And if they say no, we band together and just take what we want. They are sluts and whores, what gives them the right to say 'no'? What is one more partner?"

Brian looked at that post aghast. He thought about Alison and how she had talked with him after Chad left. He had thought he might have seen the same loneliness in her eyes that he felt in his soul. The idea of someone doing these things to her left him pale and shaky.

As admin, he had the right to turn off commenting. His hand hovered over the keypad as he tried to decide what to do. He could understand the frustration of the fellow incels and their support that his failure to pick up women was not his fault helped him feel better. The idea of having a right to a woman made him feel powerful. Until he read that last comment again and thought about the idea of using force to give you that right.

Instead of shutting down the comments, he decided to add a comment.

"There was one good thing that happened. After all that stuff, a girl from work showed up. She talked with me for a while. She was sweet and funny and seemed to really like talking to me. I really think she might be into me and maybe I could get a date set up with her."

Brian sent the post and waited. He thought his post would calm down the group by giving the guys hope. However, as soon as the messages began pouring in, it was obvious that did not work.

"Don't fall for it. It's a set up."

"She's just pretending."

"She is only going to make you look bad."

Brian read through the messages with dismay. He admitted to himself many of those things he had been already thinking, but he had hoped he was wrong. The feedback from the guys seemed to be confirming his worse fears. Alison had just been leading him on. She was never going to go out with him. Who had he been fooling?

Brian sat in despair as he watched the messages continued to role in. As they progressed, they again got more and more violent. Brian saw a post from TakeTheBlackPill again.

"You should take her. Take what you want. Don't worry about dates. They are just a trick to get you to spend money while they mess with your head over something they are never going to give you. Take it. If she complains, just kill her."

Brian blanched as he read it. He hit the kill switch and stopped all the comments and replies. He knew that would anger the other men, but he could not have death threats on his board. What if something happened to Alison? He felt his stomach churn at the thought that one of guys would figure out who she was and go after her.

These thoughts had barely gone through his mind when he started getting notifications that his messages were filling up. He knew it would be mostly from the forum members upset because he shut down posting. He closed out of it all, shut his computer down, and headed to bed. He just could not handle dealing with any more tonight. He made a mental note to make sure to review his postings and scrub anything that might reference Alison to protect her. But for now he was going to bed. Maybe things would look better in the morning.

Chapter Five

Brian woke up the next morning to his alarm buzzing. He reached over, hit the snooze, and tried to settle back down in his covers. He felt groggy and could not get his mind to focus. Laying there he thought over the night before. He was going to have to do something about his forum. The messages they posted had gone too far. But Brian did not have the heart to shut them down completely. The other men on there were the only ones that really seemed to know him.

As his alarm buzzed again, Brian shut it off and stumbled to the bathroom. He was going to need to pull himself together before he got to work. He needed to look sharp today in case he could follow up with Alison. Maybe she really meant it last night.

An hour later, Brian sat down at his computer desk in his cubicle. Brian's workspace was impersonal. The desk had a phone, a computer, and two baskets. One was for the invoices to enter and the other one was for work that had been completed. The computer system was older, but efficient for the job. However, it was prone to being slow and sluggish. Brian sighed as he looked into the to do basket. He could tell it was going to be one of those days. Three different folders of orders were already there. Each folder represented a different system he would have to get into and then out of to go to the next system. Entering the data was slow enough without having to constantly change systems.

Brian adjusted his chair and logged into the computer. He could hear his neighbor next door already keying in today's data. Brian picked up the folder out of his to do basket and opened it to the first page. The work was not hard. Just tedious. Each page had several different screens he had to page through as he entered the information into the computer. That would have been mindless enough, but with the lag as the computer switched screens, boredom would set in.

The information he inputted into the system would be used for tracking orders and inventory. It would also be analyzed for trends so the company could change their marketing and inventory to match what they predicted consumers would be buying in the upcoming weeks and months. It could all be very interesting, if he could just get a promotion to data analyst. Not to mention than he would be moved into an office and be closer to Alison. Alison had gotten promoted six months ago with the promotion he had thought would be his.

Brian spent much of the morning working on the initial three folders of orders. He had just completed them when Jerry pushed his cart through the aisle, stopping at different cubicles handing out more folders. When Jerry reached his cubicle, he placed four folders in his basket.

"Hey, Brian. I was supposed to let you know these all need done by the end of the day today."

Brian paused what he was doing and looked at Jerry. "Are you kidding me?" he asked. "Is my computer going to suddenly move at warp speed?"

Jerry smiled and cocked his head to the right. "I was just told to tell you. Don't shoot the messenger."

Brian stared at Jerry. His muddy brown eyes boring into Jerry's light brown ones. Jerry tried to hold his gaze, but couldn't. Lowering his eyes, he wiped his face and stated, "I know it is a lot. But you are our best guy. Look each one is really not that thick. I am sure you can do it."

Brian pushed back from his desk and shifted his chair so that it faced Jerry more directly. He reached for the folders and looked at each one. Tossing them into his to do pile, he stated, "I will do what I can do, but I'm not staying late unless I'm paid. Is overtime approved?"

Jerry grinned and shrugged his shoulders. "You know the rules. No overtime. I know you will do your best."

Brian turned back to his screen as Jerry left. *Best guy*, he thought. *Until it's time for a promotion*. When Brian had tried for the last data analyst position that opened up a few months ago, they had not even considered him. The rumor around the company was that Alison was on the fast track. Brian used to see her every day. They would take break together or grab coffee at the beginning of the shift. But he rarely got to see her now. Now the bosses were pushing him harder and harder.

Do four more folders today. He didn't care what they wanted he was going to take a break. Brian shook his head and pushed back hard from his desk. He stood up and walked towards the break room, stretching as he walked. He blamed his weight and poor fitness on too much sitting at work. At night, between VR and the message boards, he sat even more. He really needed to make sure to walk around now and again, he thought.

Brian shoved the door and stomped into the room before he realized that someone was already in there. Brian noticed the person as he turned towards the coffee pot. She was short and slender, with silky caramel colored hair tightly pinned up in a chignon. As she turned, the lighting picked up hints of reds and darker browns. Brian caught the flash of her short pert nose and his eyes met her hazel eyes. Her smile brightened as she recognized him.

"Brian," she said. "I wondered if I would see you today."

He had almost not recognized her. She had dressed much less conservatively when she worked in data entry and the difference between today and last night had confused him. She was dressed in a very austere business suit with a pencil skirt. Her button-down shirt was buttoned up to the top of its high collar. The jacket was tailored to be pulled in tightly at the waist and held closed with only one button. The effect was figure hugging while at the same time giving the appearance of being very matronly.

Brian instantly stood taller and stopped raking his eyes up and down her. He tried to regain his composure as he recognized her. "Alison, I didn't expect to see you here. I almost didn't recognize you. You seem so different."

Alison's smile seemed to light up even more as she moved towards him and put her hand on his forearm. "I thought I would stop by and see how everyone is doing. Seeing you last night, made me realize how long it has been since I saw anyone down here. It seems things have not changed much."

Brian reached around her for the coffee pot and bumped into her. "Excuse me," he mumbled.

Alison stepped to the side and leaned against the counter, but still stayed close enough to Brian he could almost feel her breath on his shoulder as she talked. Brian grabbed the pot and moved away. Pouring his coffee, he walked over to the only table in the break room. He pulled the chair around so he could sit and face Alison.

"You seemed upset when you walked in here," she said, as she brought her coffee over and sat down across from Brian.

"It's nothing."

Alison leaned forward and again touched him laying her hand along his on the table. "I don't think it was nothing. You looked very upset."

Brian froze. He hardly dared to move or breathe. She was touching him. What now? Brian slowly exhaled. He kept his eyes on his coffee cup.

"It is just they keep upping how many orders we have to put in every day. I just got overwhelmed for a minute. It's no big deal. I just need to get some coffee and then I will be back at it." Brian's words all rushed out at once.

Alison slowly moved her little finger up and down so that it slightly brushed against Brian's little finger and hand. She leaned farther forward perching on the edge of her seat.

"I know they have upped the workload. But I'm sure that is only because they have confidence in you."

Brian looked up through his bangs and back down at his coffee. Slightly raising his head, he stated, "They don't have so much confidence in me as to give me a promotion."

Alison pulled her hand back. Her whole attitude shifted. She became more business-like and distant. "Well, I didn't know you still were upset about that."

Brian could almost kick himself. He had ruined it. She had come here looking for him. Now he had made her upset. The silence began to stretch out uncomfortably as Brian's thoughts raced and he could not think what to say.

Suddenly Alison's face lit up as she smiled at him again. "It's okay. I know you really wanted that promotion. I just had hoped we could still be friends."

"W-w-w-we c-c-can," Brian stammered. He tried to reach across the table to hold her hand and knocked his coffee cup over. Coffee flew everywhere. Alison's quick reflexes kept her from getting any on her as she jumped up.

Brian knocked over his chair as he jumped up and moved back. He rushed to the sink, grabbing paper towels to clean up the mess. As he turned, he saw Alison moving towards the door.

"Wait," he cried, "it was good to see you."

Alison looked back over her shoulder. "It was nice to see you. We really should get together sometime. I will message you."

Brian watched her leave. He had ruined it. Once again he had no luck with a girl.

Brian put the final paper in his out basket and sat back in his chair. He had got all the orders in. He was ready to log off and go home. As he reached to shut the computer down, he noticed he had an interoffice message. Clicking to open it, he saw a short note.

Seeing you last night did really remind me of how much I have missed getting together with the gang. I can't remember the last time we went out and did something. I hope we can get the whole gang together again soon.

It was signed A. Brian sat there staring at the message for a long time before he finally shut his computer down.

Chapter Six

Brian instantly started booting up his computer system the minute he walked in the door. He had to get on the forum and tell the guys. They were not going to believe it. A girl wanted to go out with him. As he waited on the computer, he went in his room and changed into sweats and a t-shirt. Coming out, he noticed a sparkling gold icon on the lower right of his screen. He had never seen anything like it before.

Brian hesitated to click on it. He had one of the best anti-virus programs, but you could never be too careful. Hovering the cursor over it, the words "VIP invitation from Chad Williams" appeared. Brian shook his head and clicked on it. Instantly, a golden ticket appeared on the center of his screen. The ticket looked just like an old-fashioned movie ticket. The background was golden with flowing black script lettering. On each side running vertically were the words "Admit One."

The center of the ticket stated:

THIS ALLOWS ONE ENTRY TO
THE RED DOOR SALOON
VIP

FULL VR GEAR ONLY
PRESS HERE TO ENTER

Brian stared at the ticket. What had Chad done? He instantly hit his phone app and placed a video call. It rang several times. When Chad finally answered it, it was clear that he was using his bathroom mirror as his screen. Chad was standing there in nothing but a towel. Naked from the waist up, Chad's chiseled abs and flat stomach highlighted his physique. He was applying product to his hair as he systematically pulled some up into short little spikes and smoothed other areas down.

Brian watched Chad perplexed. "What are you doing?"

Chad made eye contact with Brian. "Do you think this naturally tousled hair just happens naturally? This takes work. You know if you put some effort into it, you could make your hair look better. I should send you the details for my stylist." Chad leaned towards the mirror resuming his hair styling.

Brian started to sputter. "Wh-wh-wh what-" but then stopped. He shook his head. He was not going to get into a discussion about this now. He took a breath to clear his thoughts. More focused, Brain got back on track. "I didn't call you to discuss hair tips. I called you to ask about what you sent me."

Chad stopped again. Grinning widely, he stated, "You got it, did you? I wondered. Did you use it yet? Everything is completely confidential, so I won't know if you did. Heck, I didn't even know if you opened it."

Brain asked again, "But what is it?"

Chad smiled even bigger making both his dimples pop into existence. He gave a wink of emerald green eyes. "I told you I had something special for you."

Brian waited for more information, watching as Chad started to apply shaving cream and shave his face. When he realized that Chad wasn't going to give any more information, he began to get frustrated. It was just like Chad to play coy and refuse to answer his question directly. Brian could hear Chad's voice in his head, "always leave them wanting more so they will keep coming back." Why did he have to play his salesman tricks on him. Brian could feel his face redden as his anger continued to rise.

Chad seemed to recognize that he was pushing Brian too far. He wiped his face and then leaned back from the mirror. "Okay, okay, I will explain."

"Explain then," Brian pushed.

Chad wiped his face. "The Red Door Saloon is a VR club." Chad held up his hand as Brian started to open his mouth. "Wait," he said. "You wanted me to explain. Let me explain."

"The Red Door is set up like an Old West brothel. Exactly like an Old West brothel. It is designed for you to have sex in VR with VR constructs." Chad paused. "Well, I guess it's possible you might hook up with a real person since it's almost impossible to tell constructs from avatars. Who knows maybe someone wants to have the VR experience of being an Old West prostitute."

Chad paused thinking about the scenario he had created in his own mind. Brian stated, "Go on."

Chad tilted his head as if finishing a final thought and then looked back at Brian. "Where was I? Oh yes, so basically it is a sex club. You have different levels of experience and I signed you up for the most intense. It gives you a full body experience. In fact, it is so good, I have been told the experience is even better than real world sex."

Brian felt his face flush redder and redder as he listened to Chad. Part embarrassment. Part anger. Part shame. Even his best friend thought he was hopeless. Brian lashed out, "Sex in VR! What do you think I am some sort of loser! What do you think? Poor Brian, he's never going to get a girl. This is the best he can do? Seriously, Chad! I thought you were my friend."

Chad stepped back from the mirror. He looked at Brian. "I paid good money for that ticket. Use it. Don't use it. I don't care. As I told you, it is so confidential I will never know. But, Brian, I can't take it anymore. Your constant moping about how you never get lucky. Your obsession with every girl you meet and how you can score with her. You try too hard. You push too much. I just thought if you had sex even one time, it might stop this obsession.

"Then you would be more able to relax when we go out. Enjoy the night. Not be so focused on women and how you appear to them. It might actually help you have fun. Everything in life is not about getting the girl. Sometimes, I think the only reason you spend time with me is so that I can help you get the girl."

Brian snapped, "Well that's all easy for you to say. You score whenever you want. The best closer in town with sales and girls. Don't worry, I won't be such a burden on you. I don't need to hang with you."

Chad looked at Brian. His thoughts started spinning. He had never meant to say so much. But now that it was said, he could not take it back. Brian would never believe him.

"Look Brian. I meant it to be a gift. I didn't mean to upset you. I just thought...." Chad trailed off.

"You didn't think. That's the problem. You know that some people have sex in VR and then they are addicted."

Chad snorted. "Brian, that is just an urban legend. A friend of friend of a neighbor sort of thing. No one that has sex in VR gets addicted."

Brian kept on stubbornly. "How do you know. I read about it. I have read how it traps men so that they just want VR sex and then women don't have to give it to them any more. It's just one big trap. You set me up."

Chad laughed loudly. "I never thought you for the paranoid type. Like I said if I had thought it would upset you, I would never have done it."

Brian huffed. "You never thought about how I would feel to know you think so little of me."

Chad tried to inject, "Brian, it's not that I think so little of you. I was really trying to be nice."

"Forget it. Don't worry about me. I will figure out what to do without any help from you," Brian stated. He waved his hand, clearing his screen and ending the call.

Brian sat back in his seat. Even Chad thought he was a loser. Someone that he just invited to hang out of pity. It really was true. He was never going to have a real date. Never have a real girlfriend.

Never going to have sex with a real woman. Staring at the ticket still in the middle of his screen, he tried to decide what to do. Brian closed the ticket. Looking at the golden icon at the bottom of his screen, he opened his message forum. He would talk to the guys. Why did he even bother with Chad? He would never know what it was like to be rejected. Or fear that you would never get a date. The only people who really understood him and his life were the guys on the boards.

Chapter Seven

Brian logged into his forum. He could see that several different complaints, emails, and other business items were waiting for him. But he bypassed them. Plenty of time later to deal with them. He wasn't going to be doing anything else tonight. He opened a new topic. What to write? Should he tell them about Alison. Should he tell them about Chad's ticket. Remembering the violent posts from last night, he added a to-do item on the admin side to make sure he scrubbed all of Alison's personal references from his posts. He also reminded himself that he needed to take care not to give out too much information.

I saw that girl from last night. She talked to me about getting together sometime. She said she missed seeing me around. I used to see her every day. But now I don't. We sat and drank coffee together. I was so surprised she touched me twice. The first time she put her hand on my arm as she greeted me. The second time she placed her hand near mine and rubbed her finger along my hand. I think she might like me. I don't know. She is so beautiful. She messaged me wanting to get together some time soon. I just don't know what to do.

Brian reviewed what he posted. It seemed clear who he was discussing, without giving away any information that could be used to track down who he was talking about. He sent the post and started his admin duties. He could see where more violent posts had been made. Several group members had flagged them for his review. He was going to have to decide what to do about these members before they got more out of control. But not today.

Brian worked on his various admin tasks with his notifications turned off. He knew that if he started hearing the chime he would be tempted to look at what the guys were posting. However, he also knew he needed to tidy up his site. He had threads to archive, complaints to review, and most of all he needed to check on what personal information he had posted in the past. After he completed the tasks, he turned back on his notifications. Time to see what had been posted.

Brian was not surprised to see several watch out posts again.

"I still say this is a trap."

"She's just playing you."

"I don't care if she messaged you, don't fall for it."

Brian could see that point of view. That was why he had posted this in the first place. He had some of the same thoughts and wanted to see what others would think. But he was pleased to see that some of the other posts were giving him encouragement.

"She did message you. That has to mean something."

"She went out of her way to see you. Touched you twice. Then messaged you. What are you waiting for? Call her."

He could see how thread wars had broken out between the two sides with each replying back to the other's posts trying to make their points. The posts that gave him the most confidence were the ones that discussed how her behavior was likely a signal that she was interested in sex.

TooLonely had written, "She touched you twice, bro! Why are you talking to us? You need to follow up and get some. Take one for the team and have some sex. It is time for you to stop being an incel if only for a moment."

NeverAgain24 had answered, "You really think this is going

anywhere. She is probably just having pity on him and thinks he's too stupid to know."

TooLonely had replied, "Wish someone had pity on me like that. Sex is sex. Even pity sex is better than no sex. It's not like they are getting married or anything."

Brian stared at those last words thoughtfully. He was not sure what he thought about having sex with Alison. Yeah, it would be great, he told himself. But was that really where their relationship was? He hadn't seen her in at least three weeks before last night. Now after two brief encounters, he was going to have sex with her?

Brian found himself instinctively starting to call Chad. No, he was not calling him. Not after the sex ticket and their fight. He pulled his hand back, tapping his fingers on his desk. Who could he call? Someone that would help him break the mental tie in his head between going forward with Alison and pulling back until she made the next move. Someone that would help him know how fast to move. Inspiration struck. He needed a woman's perspective. He would call Susan.

Chapter Eight

Brian screened Susan. He was just about to end the call when she answered. Susan was squinting at the screen as she fumbled for her glasses. Susan struggled with poor eyesight and her thick glasses dominated her face once she put them on. Brian was always amazed how her glasses transformed her sky blue eyes from being large and framed by luscious lashes to being small and barely noticeable. He always wondered why she never got contacts or had eye surgery. She was so beautiful in a classic sense without them. But with them the black oversized frames overpowered her delicate face, drawing the eye until the only thing you noticed were her old, very dark, very thick, very heavy glasses and how small they made her eyes.

Susan got her glasses on and blinked a few times as her eyes focused. She stopped squinting, but her eyes still seemed small and close set behind her lenses. "Brian, I don't think I have talked to you in ages. It is good to see you."

Brian smiled slightly bashfully. He felt bad that he did not keep in touch with Susan more since high school. She had started working right out of school while he went to college. He really did not have much reason to shop in a women's high-end chic clothing store. He knew it was an excuse. Thinking about it made him realize that his life was slowly being consumed by his time on his forum. In fact, his night out with Chad last night was the first time he had been in VR in weeks. The last time had been at Chad's insistence also. When was the last time he had been out in the real world other than work, he wondered.

"Hey, Susan. I don't have much excuse except I just don't ever get out anymore. I work. I'm home. I sleep. Pretty boring and basic."

Susan gave a small smile tilting her head to one side. "You still could call. You know that does not take much work."

Brian gave a weak chuckle and agreed. "Like I said, no excuses. I just find myself sitting around here much of the time doing nothing. It is just a bad, boring routine."

Susan pursed her rose bud lips and blew out. "I guess I can forgive you," she stated teasing Brian.

Brian decided he better make some small talk before he jumped in and asked for her advice. It was bad enough he had not talked to her in forever. "How has business been?" he asked.

Susan giggled. "You know you don't care one bit about women's fashion."

"I know I don't care, but I do care about how your store is doing because it is your store."

Susan's smile grew bigger. "I have been working on trying to guess trends and use some influencers to push my guesses. The results have been mixed, but I think I have gotten a market share for my store that is likely to keep me stable."

Brian just stared at Susan, not having a clue how to respond.

Susan caught his blank smile and shook her head. "Sorry. I get so used to talking shop with others, I forget that not everyone understands.

"A boutique like mine lives or dies on staying relevant. That means it has to have the latest trends and fashions. But you have to be careful or you end up buying lots of clothes that you can't sell because the trends change so fast. However, if you just follow the trends, you risk no one wanting to shop at your place because you are seen as out of touch."

Susan paused to see if Brian was following. He gave a slight nod and gestured for her to continue.

"So, you have to guess them. But that is risky. Guess wrong and you could lose lots of money. Or in my case, I could cost the store lots of money and lose my job. So, I have been watching trends and then I try and find influencers to wear the trends I buy."

Brian's face became confused again. "Influencers?"

Susan answered, "Influencers are people that other people follow. So, if a famous model or celebrity that is known for being fashionable wears a specific outfit, soon everyone wants one like it. Or at least similar to it. It is a way to try and control the market, not just follow it."

Brian thought for a minute. "That is pretty smart. It is almost what our data analyst do. They look at orders to try and determine what is going to be ordered next week or even the week after."

Susan nodded. "Yes, but then take it one step farther and after you bank on those orders, you get someone to place an order forcing others to want to order also."

Brian looked at Susan. He was amazed at how sharp her mind was. She had learned how to try and predict and manage something as capricious as fashion trends without using data and analysis. She had not even gone to college. His admiration for what she was doing came out in his voice, "Susan that is amazing."

Susan's cheeks turned a delicate pink and she tilted her head forward while looking up at him through her golden waves of hair. "You really think so. I just read fashion magazines and subscribed to designer blogs. Anyone could do it."

"No really, you take all that and you put all the pieces together and you get an answer no one else gets. That is just …. I don't know that I can think of any other word… Amazing."

Brian and Susan stared at each other through their screens until Brian reminded himself why he had called. "Susan, did you ever meet my co-worker Alison?"

Susan sat straighter, brow furrowed. "I'm not sure. I think I might have. You invited some work people the last time I went out with you and Chad. I'm pretty sure she was one of them."

Brian nodded. "Yes, I think you are right. Anyway, she got a promotion so I don't see her much at work anymore. I bumped into her at a VR club Chad drug to me to the other night."

Susan interrupted, "You are still letting Chad drag you to those things? I would have thought you were finally able to stand up to him by now. They really aren't your thing."

Brian leaned back, hurt by her statement. "I.. well, I.... Ummm." Brian was not sure what to say. Deciding to ignore her comments he continued.

"She then went out of her way to stop by my office today. I was having coffee with her when I spilled mine. As I cleaned up, she had to get back to work. But she messaged me later saying she wants to meet up. So, I don't know what to do. Should I call her? Should I message her? Should I ask her out? How many times should I go out with her before I have..." Brian blurted out breaking off before he could completely embarrass himself.

Susan stared at him, her lips thinned and her eyes hard behind her glasses. "Before you what?"

Brian mumbled and looked down refusing to make eye contact.

Susan asked again, "Before you do what?"

Brian continued to stare at his lap avoiding her through the screen. Maybe he should have just emailed her. Or called the old-fashioned way with no video. Maybe he should have just went to bed and not even bothered.

Susan's voice sharpened, "Brian, did you call me to ask me how soon you can ask another girl for a booty call? Did you seriously call me because you wanted tips on how to date another girl without any thought to me or how it might make me feel? Seriously, why are you not calling Chad about this?"

Brian peeked a glance up at Susan dropping his eyes quickly back down. "Chad and I are fighting."

Susan's voice became shrill, "So, I was not even your first choice on how to make a booty call!"

Brian refused to answer or look up. He could tell Susan was upset, but was not sure why. To him, she had always just been one of the guys. He had never really thought about her being a girl.

Besides, she wasn't interested in him, so why would she care if he hooked up with another girl?

Susan took a deep breath and lowered her tone enunciating every word very carefully and slowly. "If you want advice on a booty call with some other girl do not call me again. If you want to talk to me about me or spend time with me, then you can call. I thought you respected me more than this. It would have been better if you were calling me for a booty call."

Somehow Susan signed off with a click that made it sound like slamming down an old-fashioned phone. Brian jerked in his seat and sighed. He had blown it again.

Chapter Nine

Brian sat at his desk the next day, trying to bury himself in the numbers. He couldn't concentrate. The screens kept blurring as he stared at them too long without doing any input. He was getting farther and farther behind on the day's work. He started to shove back from his desk, when the memo icon caught his eye. Deciding to take the plunge, he sent a message back to Alison.

> Alison
>
> So sorry about spilling the coffee. As you can tell, I'm still the klutz. But I think it would be great if we all got together and went out. I know the last time we did anything we went bowling. Not sure if you would be up for that. I have had enough VR for a while, I'm thinking the real world? Let me know what you think.
>
> Brian

After sending it, Brian felt ice cold and feverishly hot at the same time. His hands started shaking and he could not see what he was doing. Instantly, he doubted that he had made the right decision. She was going to have a good laugh when she got it. Not anything he could do now. It was done.

Brian looked at the clock. Gathering up his coat and items, he decided to take lunch out so he would not have to wait for the return message telling him 'no'. Or worse yet, no response at all. He called out to Jerry, "I'm headed out for lunch. Back in 30 minutes."

Jerry responded, "You don't look so hot. You seem kind of pale. Are you sure you aren't sick?"

"No, just low blood sugar probably," he covered. "I didn't eat a very good breakfast. I'm going to go fuel up now so I can get more done this afternoon."

Jerry nodded. "Get yourself something nutritious. Low blood sugar is nothing to mess with. I once had a friend end up in the hospital with it."

Brian gave Jerry a look as he walked past. Jerry was a large built guy. At over six feet, he was the tallest person on the floor. Broad shoulders and no neck made him look like he could be a linebacker. But the years had not been kind to Jerry. He was slowly growing a paunch that resulted in him having to constantly hitch up his slacks when he assigned work and gathered the completed entries. He also seemed like he might have been tackled one or more times too many. But he was sweet and had a kind smile for everyone. Sometimes though, Brian just was not sure about the things he said.

"Don't worry, Jerry, I will make sure and eat well," Brian reassured him as he put his hand on his shoulder. "I'm sure I will be fine."

Jerry smiled back at Brian and said, "That's good, because it sure would be no fun going bowling without you, if you weren't there?"

Brian walked towards the elevator as he processed what Jerry had just said. He reached to push the down button and froze. Turning slowly, he asked, "What did you just say, Jerry?"

"I just don't think bowling would be as much fun without you."

"Jerry, what bowling?" Brian asked.

Jerry lost his smile, his face going blank. "Forget I said anything. No one told me it was surprise. Now I ruined the surprise. Alison will be so mad at me."

Brian walked back towards Jerry. "No one is going to be mad at you. Just tell me what Alison said. I know about the bowling. I just seem to be confused on some of the details," Brian spoke soothingly and calmly to Jerry.

Jerry pointed to his computer. "I got a message. A bunch of us did. It was from Alison. She said how she bumped into you and the two of you talked old times. She said how she told you she missed all of us. You thought it would be a good idea for us to all get together like we used to and go bowling. She even had a winking face and a smiling face at the end. Did the winking face mean to keep it a secret?"

Brian turned to hurry back to his computer. She thought everyone was going. On their date. Oh no. "This cannot be happening. This cannot be happening," Brian chanted under his breath as he hurried back to his computer. Maybe it was not too late to fix this.

Brian booted up his computer, ignoring Jerry's questions about his lunch. He watched as his messages icon lit up. Clicking on it he found that Alison had answered him and then sent out a message to several of their mutual work friends. He groaned as he realized it was too late.

Hey Brian,

No worries about the coffee. I would love to have us all go out. I will send out an invite to all the usual people. I don't have a way to message Chad now that he's not working here. Can you make sure he knows? Say Friday night. 7 pm. I agree meeting in the real world will be so much more fun.

A

The message was followed by cute invites she had made with the date, time and location. By his count, it appeared she had invited at least 15 people, 16 if he counted Chad. Chad. How was he going to invite Chad? He wasn't even speaking to him right now. Maybe he could still stop this.

Alison

That sounds great. I was thinking more a small group going. Or maybe even just me and you? But I don't know. Anyway, I'm sure I can reach Chad right now. Let me know what you think about just you and me.

Brian

This was not going the way he had planned it at all. He was going to have to figure out a way to spend time with Alison alone.

He heard the computer chime. Sure enough, another message from Alison.

Brian

I guess I thought you meant all of us. Sorry. But everyone is so excited about coming, I just can't tell them no now. Maybe we can go another time. Jerry already messaged me and asked how many games we are going to play. I don't have the heart to tell him 'no'. I think I have Chad's number. I will just call him.

A

Brian leaned over and peered out of his cubicle, down the aisle to Jerry's desk. He could see him talking to another data entry clerk. He was laughing and smiling discussing how he was going to dig out his old bowling shoes and go "real time bowling". Pulling back into his cubicle, Brian put his head in his hands. He didn't know what he was going to do now.

"I guess I am just going to have to live with it. Maybe next time I will be able to make it just the two of us. I will have to be clearer," he said to himself. Rubbing his face to clear his thoughts, he grabbed his coat. He'd better go get lunch now. Maybe he would luck out and Alison would not be able to reach Chad.

Brian got home that night tired and frustrated. He felt as if as usual any chance he had with the girl was slipping through his fingers. He started to log into his forum and stopped. What was the point? He knew he had failed again. He didn't need someone else telling him that. What would be the point? The guys were great, but they were never going to help him get a girl.

Brian took his fingers off the keys, staring at the computer. Glancing down, he looked at the golden ticket. Thoughts flashed through his mind. Maybe he should give it a try. He would not have to tell Chad. In fact, it would be better if he never told Chad. But what if he got addicted? Could you really get addicted from one time? Maybe he should find out more before he just threw away this opportunity.

A few hours later, Brian was in the middle of research on the Red Door Saloon, sex clubs in general, VR sex clubs, and sex addictions. He was beginning to feel he was on information overload when his incoming call alert lit up. Hastily, he killed all his windows even though he knew they would not be able to see what he was researching. He was in such a hurry, he accepted the call without even realizing who it was. When Chad's face popped up on the screen, Brian felt his heart rate shoot up. He really did not need this tonight.

"Hey, Brian. I am glad to see you are not still mad at me," Chad started the conversation.

Brian as was typical with Chad felt three steps behind. "I don't know what you mean."

"Alison. She called me. Said you and the gang were going bowling. Invited me along. I figured it had to be your idea. I barely know her."

Brian swallowed hard. Trying to buy some time, he grabbed his drink. *Think fast, think fast*, he thought. "Yeah, I..well….she….well…. Yes."

Chad stared at Brian, "Yes, what?"

Brian tried again. "Yes you are invited. But actually it was Alison's idea. I wasn't sure if you would be interested. I know bowling and the real world is not your thing. You don't have to come. I will let Alison know."

Chad snorted, "So you are still mad at me. Whatever. Not sure how much fun it is going to be Friday if you are going to just stammer and be a jerk. But it sounds like a blast. See you Friday."

Chad signed off leaving Brian alone with his computer again. He was getting used to getting hung up on. Maybe it was time to find something else to do and spend less time online.

Chapter Ten

The week seemed to drag on and on to Brian. It was as if Friday would never arrive. Then, quite suddenly, it was here. The data entry that day seemed especially tedious. Each folder seemed to have too many entries. The clock hands moved as if they were moving through molasses. Then, just as suddenly as the day had arrived, the end of the day came. Brian packed up his things, shut his computer down and hurried out the door. Arriving home, he took care in how he got ready.

Fresh from the shower, he tried to tousle and twist his hair the way he had seen Chad doing his. His hair just ended up hanging in tangled knots looking as if he had knotted a horse's tail and placed it on his head. Yanking the comb through his hair, he pulled it out straight and gave up. It hung limply around his round face, making it look even more moon like. His eyes were wide and dark, looking like two circles in the bigger circle of his face.

Brian looked at himself in the mirror, remembering how Chad had seemed so strong and yet slender when he had screened him. Brian knew he could not compare. His puffy arms hung from his rounded shoulders. His chest looked more like pillows of rising bread than muscles. His stomach rounded out slightly creating a slight bulge at his waist. Even the steam from his shower could not hide the shape.

Brian angrily turned from the mirror, walking to his closet. He was not Chad. He was never going to be Chad. He should just stop comparing himself to Chad. He found a comfortable pair of blue jeans, some Converse sneakers, and a T-shirt. He was sure Chad would come in some sharp outfit, but he was not Chad. Besides, why should he compete against Chad. It was him Alison had sought out. He just needed to stay focused on her. Nothing else.

Brian walked into the bowling alley greeting his co-workers as he saw them. Jerry was showing off his shoes he had found at the back of his closet. Another clerk, Sarah, was standing at the ball rack trying to find one that would fit her hand with the assistance of a manager, Tom. Brian waved to them as he walked over to find a ball for himself.

"This is a great idea, Brian," Sarah commented, "maybe we should do this on a regular basis. It would be fun. We could even think about a league team."

Brian nodded not really listening. "Sure, Sarah. Have you seen Alison?"

Sarah looked around. "I just saw her. She was setting up scoring sheets. She had that guy with her."

Brian got nervous. "What guy?"

"You know your friend. The one that worked in the mail room before he took some other job. The blond yummy one."

Brian whirled around looking at the lanes. The group was clustered on the first four lanes to the right of the whole alley. People were dividing into four groups. Two groups playing as a teams against each other on each set of two lanes. Sure enough in the middle of it was Alison. Brian watched as her natural leadership and grace came through as she handed out scoring sheets and directed people. Brian smiled as he admired her beauty. He really could look at her all night.

Then, his gaze drifted to the right. Chad was standing to the right and slightly behind Alison. He was clapping people on the back, laughing, and being one of the guys. Brian frowned. This was not how he wanted things to go.

Brian grabbed a ball with little care and marched over the lanes. "Hey, Alison," he called louder than he expected.

Everyone turned to look at him. Alison flushed slightly. "Brian, I didn't see you come in. Let's get you on a team."

As Alison turned to put Brian's name on a score sheet, Brian saw Chad mouth, "You're late," over Alison's shoulder. Brian just glared at him. Trying to ease closer to Alison, Brian bumped into one of the other workers.

"Hey, watch where you are going. These seats are all taken."

Alison looked up at the commotion and frowned at Brian. "I'm sorry. It looks like the only openings are on the teams on lane 4. But after the first game, we can switch up." She patted Brian on the arm. "It will be okay."

Brian let Alison steer him towards the group she was assigning him to in bewilderment. How was he getting moved all the way over here away from her, when this had all been his idea? Well not all of it. This was way more people than he wanted here. But the overall concept was his idea.

Brian sat down and started putting on his shoes. At the sound of loud laughter, he looked up. He saw Chad sitting by Alison, his arm loosely around her shoulders. It was obvious that he had been telling a story. Both sides of the table were focused on him and listening. He gave another punch line and they all started laughing. Brian turned away. It was going to be a long night.

When the games started, Alison took the scorekeeper's seat in Lane 1. From his seat on Lane 4, Brian could look directly over to her. He sat watching as each time Chad bowled, he would stop and touch Alison. Bending down to talk directly into her ear. Leaning against her. Brushing against her. He knew Chad's moves. It was painful as he watched Chad pull every single one and Alison was eating it all up.

Finally, Brian turned away. He sat fuming the rest of his game.

He barely spoke to any of the people on his team. Every time another burst of laughter came from the other lane, Brian sulked more. He started bowling poorly with his anger, which just frustrated him more. It was just like the clubs, but only worse. These were supposed to be his friends, his co-workers, in a place that was his type of place. Why did Chad just take over and ruin everything? Brian kept counting the frames until the game would be done.

Brian could see when the other game got done when his had one frame left. The people broke up. Some went to the bar to get drinks. Others went to the bathroom or to get food. It was his turn to bowl. When he walked back to his seat, he realized that Alison was no longer at the other table. Looking around, he did not see her anywhere. He started to walk off and go find her, when the ball return spit out his ball. He had to bowl one last time. He quickly walked to the end of the lane, released the ball, and walked away. Not even waiting to see what he scored.

Brian reached the bar, but did not see Alison there. He turned to Jerry. "Do you know where Alison went?"

The big guy grinned, "This is so much fun. I don't know why we ever stopped having these get togethers."

Brian ground his teeth. "Yes. So much fun. Where is Alison?"

"Oh, I think she went outside. Something about it being too hot in here and needing to cool down."

Brian headed to the front door. He could hear his group whooping as their game finally ended. He really didn't care how it went, he just wanted to make sure that he found Alison. He had to make sure he was on her team the next round. As he was walking to the door, Sarah called out to him, "We won Brian. Aren't you excited?"

Brian paused. "That's great, Sarah. But I am headed outside. I will be back in a minute."

Sarah's face crumpled. She lowered her head, so that her dirty blond hair fell in her face. "Oh, I just thought-. Well, I... I mean some of us were getting a drink to celebrate. I thought, you-. Well, never mind." Sarah pushed her eyeglasses back up on her face.

Brian looked at Sarah. She was really a nice girl. Plain in a kind of pleasing way, but still sweet. She was about a year younger than Brian, but she almost always dressed like she was someone's grandma. Tonight was no exception. She had on a full blue skirt with pockets, a short sleeve cream blouse, and a cardigan sweater that matched her skirt. She was even wearing a pearl necklace. The outfit might look retro and cute on someone like Alison, but on Sarah, it looked old and dumpy.

"Maybe in a minute. I need to make sure Alison is going to get the next game set up."

"Oh, okay," Sarah answered. She turned to the bar slowly, looking back at Brian over her shoulder. "But if you change your mind, come join us."

Brian nodded and moved out the door. The evening was cool and crisp. He took a deep breath of the night air as he looked around. He did not immediately see anyone. Brian wondered if maybe Jerry had been wrong. He took two more steps forward, peering around the dark parking lot. He was just about to go in when he heard a noise to his left. The bowling alley had a seating area to the left of the door. A wooden gazebo stood around part of it to shelter it from rain and sun. The noise seemed to be coming from the area inside where the parking lot lights did not reach.

Brian wondered what Alison could be doing in there. He hurried forward calling her name. As he moved into the gazebo, lights from the back shone through and lit up what the front had kept him from seeing. Alison and Chad were seated at a picnic table embracing. Even as Brian stopped, he could tell they were kissing deeply. Chad's hands appeared to be under Alison midriff shirt. Alison had her arms around Chad with one hand entwined in his hair and the other in the small of his back. At the sound of his voice, they pulled apart.

"Brian, what are you doing here?" Alison gasped. From the flush on her face and tremor in her voice, it was apparent they had been kissing for a while.

"Alison. I-I-I d-d-d-don't understand," Brian stammered, "I th-th-thought we were on a d-d-date."

"A date?" Alison questioned. "What date?"

"I asked you to go bowling. It was supposed to be a date."

Alison tilted her head back until her silky hair fell almost all the way to her butt. She started laughing so hard, she was soon gasping for breath. "You thought you asked me out," she gasped. "You asked me out," she paused again, "on a date." She laughed again.

Brian clenched his fists and bit his lip. He didn't know whether to yell or cry. What had gone wrong? Why was she laughing at him? How did she end up with Chad? Trying to control the quiver in his voice he stated, "I don't understand. I asked you to go bowling."

Alison wiped tears from her eyes as she got her laughing under control. "Brian, you are sweet. But I never wanted to go out with you. I just wanted an office party that Chad would come to. I wanted to connect up with him. I never said I wanted to date you. I kept saying let's all go out."

Brian felt as if he had been hit by a truck. For a second, he thought his knees were going to collapse. He actually swayed. Brian put his hand on the door frame and leaned against it for a minute. He let the wood hold him up as he muttered under his breath, "They were right. They were right. This was nothing but I set up. They were right."

Chad stood up and began to move towards Brian. "Hey buddy, who was right? What are you talking about?" Chad laid his hand on Brian's arm.

Brian jerked his arm out of Chad's grasp and stepped back. "I'm not your buddy. Just leave me alone. You take everything. You could have any woman you want. You have had all those women. Why, just why couldn't you leave this one alone? You knew I liked her. You are not my friend."

Brian jerked around and started walking towards the street. He could hear Chad calling out to him. But he kept walking. He was done. Everything the guys on the message board said was true. It was time that he just accepted he was an incel and he would be an incel forever.

Chapter Eleven

Brain had been walking for about thirty minutes when he realized that he did not know where he was going or even where he was. He was walking near a small neighborhood park. Scattered along the sidewalk were some park benches. Brian moved to the nearest one and sat down. It was late. He had left his jacket back at the bowling lanes and was getting cold. He needed to find a way to get home. He pulled his phone out of his back pocket. It was blowing up with messages. He saw he had several missed calls from Chad. A few messages from Jerry. But nothing from Alison. He wasn't surprised.

Brian cleared his notifications away. He sat with arms on his legs and his head hanging down. Susan. Her name just popped into his head. Call Susan. Brian looked at his phone with trepidation. Their last call had not gone so well. Brian thought about how he felt about Alison using him to get to Chad. Maybe that's how Susan had felt. Brian decided he would give her a call, what other option did he have right now?

"Brian, you calling to ask how to get a booty call with another girl again," Susan answered.

Brian froze. "Nn-nn-no."

Susan laughed. "It's okay. What's up?"

Brian said, "I just had a really bad night and wanted someone to talk to. Chad and I are still on the outs. I don't know. Your name just popped into my head. I know I was not very nice last time, but I just need.....," Brian trailed off, "I'm not sure what I need.

Susan looked at Brian, all humor off her face. "It sounds like you really need a friend."

Brian nodded glumly, "I really do."

Susan took pity on him, "Come on over. You can't stay too late. I have to get up tomorrow even though it's Saturday. But you can come talk for a while."

"Thank you."

Brian was nervous by the time he reached Susan's apartment. He was unsure. Here he was coming to lay his problems with another girl at her feet. How was this any different from what he did with Chad? What he did to her the last time he talked to her? Gathering up the courage to knock, Brian decided that it was different because he was being honest. He had told Susan that he needed to vent. She accepted that so it was okay.

Susan answered the door. She had her hair down and the long waves cascading down her back. She was not wearing her glasses. Brian looked at her in surprise as he realized how beautiful her face was when it was not hidden behind her heavy dark frames. His face must have reflected his shock as Susan commented, "Yes, I know. I am not wearing my glasses. A friend of mine got me to try out contacts. I'm not sure I like them."

Susan pulled the door open farther and stepped back. "Come on in."

Brian walked into her small apartment. It was cozy, but stylish. It was immediately obvious that someone with a knack for design had decorated the apartment. The living room, dining room, and kitchen were one big room, which Susan had broken up through the use of color and furniture arrangements. Each "room" had its own color scheme with knickknacks and decorative touches that matched.

The kitchen was done in a bright sunny yellow with white contrast. Curtains, hand towels, and kitchen gadgets on the counters were all done it those colors. The dining room was done in neutrals, tans, browns, and grays and placed in a way to form a boundary between the kitchen and living room colors. The living room continued the neutral color scheme, but added splashes of gold, rust, and burgundy. This created an effect of making a person think it was three separate rooms and added depth and dimension to the small apartment.

Susan moved towards the love seat. She sat down patting the cushion beside her. "Come. Sit. Let's talk," she stated.

Brian moved and sat beside her. He sat carefully down trying to ensure he stayed on his cushion and to refrain from touching her. The couch was comfortable, but cozy. Barely room for two people.

"Thank you for letting me come over. I was just so upset. I feel kind of awkward bothering you with all this," Brian stated.

Susan smiled. "Don't worry. It sounds like you had a rough night. Tell me about it."

Brian stated, "It all started with Alison. I saw her the other night when I was out with Chad."

Susan frowned. "I think I know all about this. Do we really need to go over it again?"

Brian sputtered on his next words, trying not to feel embarrassed all over again. "S-s-susan, I am really s-s-sorry about all of that."

Susan sat back against the corner and tilted her body so she was staring straight at Brian. "I know. It's okay. It just still kind of annoys me. Brian, you are a really nice guy. You just need to have confidence in yourself."

Brian stared into her clear blue eyes. He could see warmth and friendship in her tentative smile. He had never realized how truly beautiful Susan was. Or kind. As Brian thought about, it came to him that he had never really given Susan much of a thought at all. She had been put in the "friend zone" and he had never considered why.

"The next day, I saw her again at work. She said we should get together. I thought she was just being nice, but she emailed me later that day and everything," Brian started.

Susan maintained eye contact and nodded her head to encourage him to continue.

"I am not really sure what went wrong from there, I guess. I don't know. It just all went wrong."

Susan put her hand up in front of her. "Stop. Just tell me step by step."

"I emailed her back and asked her to go bowling. I was not real clear about meaning it was a date. So, I don't know if she misunderstood me or if she did it on purpose. But next thing I knew, she had invited half the data analyst employees and wanted me to invite Chad."

"Chad?" Susan interrupted.

"Yes, she knew him from when she worked with me and he used to work in the mail room. When we would have work things and parties, he would come sometimes," Brian explained. "I don't know. Looking back, it seems like she mentioned him every time we talked. I didn't notice it at the time."

"Probably because you were too busy hearing what you wanted to hear," Susan injected.

Brian dropped his head. When he looked back up the hurt showed in his dark eyes. "I probably didn't notice because I never thought someone would use me just to hook up with someone else."

Susan looked down as her face flushed. Brian stared at her profile while her face was down. She had creamy white skin that seemed as smooth as porcelain. Her high cheekbones highlighted her oval face. Without her glasses, her eyes were slightly almond shaped. He still could not believe he had never noticed her beauty.

"That was not nice of me," Susan said. "You are right. Even if you were not listening who expects someone to use them like that. Please continue."

Brian gave her a shy smile, took a deep breath, and continued. "So, the next thing I know about twenty of us are all bowling together. Alison and Chad not only on the same lane, but on the same team. I am two lanes over and not even able to talk to her.

"When we have a break between games, I go looking for her. I find her and Chad outside kissing. Well, it looked like more than kissing, but I didn't really stick around to find out.

"I stomped off and ended up in a park. I was sitting on the park bench feeling sorry for myself when I thought to call you. I just feel... I don't even know how I feel. I just know that Chad and I got in fight. I didn't even want him there. Now he is with the girl I thought I was going on a date with. The girl he knew I liked," Brian finished in a rush.

Susan sat there for a minute looking at him. "Brian, that is horrible. I thought Chad was your friend. I don't know what to say. This is really all the pits."

Susan leaned over and gave Brian a small kiss on the cheek. "You have really had a rough night. I am going to make you some tea."

Before Brian could object, Susan moved to the kitchen. Brian sagged back against the cushions and watched her making the tea. She moved with a grace that was almost hypnotic. He could tell by how little attention she paid to her actions that she had performed this task countless times before. Brian slowly felt something inside him relax as her movements soothed him. He breathed deeply, smelling hints of vanilla and lilacs. The calm and peacefulness of the room washed over him.

Brian must have closed his eyes because the next thing he knew Susan was slowly sitting down holding two cups of tea. The sight of her as he opened his eye sent a small chill through him. He took the tea, carefully so as not to spill it.

"Thank you," he commented as he gestured around the room with his other hand. "This is a really nice place you have here. I don't think I have ever been here before."

Susan shook her head. "We have screened each other, but I don't think we have seen each other in person since college."

Brian shook his head, more in disbelief than disagreement. "That can't be right."

Susan nodded.

Brian continued to stare at her. How had he missed her beauty? Her kindness? Her grace? She was a wonderful, smart, caring woman. Why had he never considered dating her? All the hours of complaining on his message boards about how women just overlook men like him and here he had been overlooking her.

Brian sat his cup down on the small end table by the couch. He took Susan's from her and placed it beside his. He reached out, taking both her hands in his. Leaning in, Brian started to kiss her on her full red lips.

Susan jerked back, standing as she moved. "Brian, what is going on? What are you doing?"

Brian sat on the couch staring up at her in confusion. "I just realized you are smart, funny, caring... I had never really thought about you in this way before. I think you are so beautiful. I just thought, maybe we could.. I don't know. I thought you liked me," he finished.

"I do like you, Brian. You have always been a great friend. And, I think you are a really great guy. But you are just a friend. I think you will make a great boyfriend for someone, but just not for me."

Brian stared at her not believing what he was hearing. Twice in one night. Could his luck get any worse? He grabbed his coat and headed to the door. Fumbling with the doorknob, he felt his face getting redder and redder. Suddenly the door gave. Not expecting it, Brian flung it open with more force than he expected and flew out of the apartment.

He could hear Susan behind him. "Brian, wait! Don't leave."

But he kept on going out into the dark, cold night.

Chapter Twelve

Brian stomped into his house slamming the door. He was cold from his long walk home. Flopping down in his chair, he went to boot up his computer. As he reached for the button, he caught a glimpse of his face reflected in the dark screen. Slowly, he turned it side to side, studying himself from various angles. Closing his eyes, he dropped back in his chair and covered his face with his hands.

Brian looked up and looked around his bleak apartment with new eyes. It compared unfavorably to Susan's. Where hers was cozy and inviting, all he saw here was coldness. His living room was not even really a living room. The wall between the living room and his bedroom was taken up completely by his desk, computer set up, and screens. The furniture was all utilitarian, black, metal, and glass.

Sitting under the window on the wall to his right was his VR couch. Continuing on around the room was a small wooden table and two chairs where he would often eat his meals. The room had no wall hangings or decorations. He had one throw rug in the middle of the floor that was a dark gray. Even the lighting in the room was sparse. One ceiling fixture and a floor lamp by his couch.

Brian looked back at his computer. Was this really all he had? The guys on the computer? How had his life gotten to this point?

Brian felt unsure of the decisions he had made recently. Sitting there, he could feel himself seeking into despair. The buzzing of his phone distracted Brian from his thoughts. He looked and saw that Susan had messaged him.

Opening his app, Brian read her text.

Brian

I am so sorry for all the confusion. I want you to know, I really like talking to you. You listen and take me seriously. So many people ignore me because "all you do is sell clothes". But you get me. I just want you to know that I hope we can still be friends. I know the perfect woman is out there for you. It just is not me. I hope you understand.

Let's have coffee soon.

Susan

Brian slammed his phone down on the computer desk. He booted up his computer and called up his messages from his phone, angrily poking the keys as he typed.

Susan

How dare you pull the "let's be friends" crap with me. I have been your friend and poured my heart out to you. Now, you say, you just don't see me that way, but hey you like talking to me? Whatever. Yes, this will most certainly impact our friendship as in now we have no friendship. So please refrain from contacting me again.

Brian

Brian's hand hovered over the send key, debating with himself. Steeling himself for the possible pain, he hit the key and sent the message. Then he pulled a KillZit program. Brian had learned from previous experiences that just because you blocked someone from calling, they could find various ways on social media to continue to contact you. He had found a program that fixed that for him.

Brian typed his name in the first box. He put Susan's name in the second. When he hit enter, the program began to systematically search for any connections he and Susan might have through social media, apps, or phone that she might use to contact him. The app then blocked her ability to do so. The status bar at the bottom showed the progress being made. Once it hit 100%, she would no longer have any access to him.

Brian guessed in theory she could look him up and come see him in person. If she did put in that much effort, maybe he would talk to her. But if he didn't feel like it, she would still be blocked if he chose to not answer the door.

When the program was done, Brian started to open the message boards, but decided not tonight. He'd had his fill of drama tonight. Two rejections were enough. He didn't need the guys telling him everything he did wrong. He knew he should never trust girls, but he did it anyway. He knew he should just give up, but he kept trying anyway. He knew women loved to lead men on, but he kept following anyway. He really should have known better, and they would tell him that. He was not up for that tonight.

The next morning – Saturday - Brian slept late. He got up and had some cereal. Staying in his gym shorts and a T-shirt, he moped around the house. Two or three times, he went to check his phone for messages, but then didn't even pick it up. Who would be leaving him any messages? Chad and Alison would not be calling him anytime soon. Susan couldn't. Brian moped more as he realized how few friends he had and that he was not speaking to almost all of them.

Brian did get on his computer in the afternoon. He had some admin duties for his forum. He did read some of the messages posted, but still didn't post any of his own. He knew that waiting would not change the outcome, but he just did not feel ready.

Late in the afternoon, a pop-up showed up on his screen. Brian sat looking at it without really comprehending. His spyware and anti-virus programs were top of the line. How did a pop-up get through? Since he had not really been on any websites, where did it come from? As he sat there thinking, his brain finally registered the message. It appeared to be an invitation for a new VR club. They must have bought a guest list from another club and were sending out invites. That explained how it got past his programs.

Another club, just what I don't need, he thought. *Another place to go and get rejected. Another place where I will stick out like a sore thumb because I don't have the right clothes, the right look, the right anything.* Even as he had been thinking these thoughts, Brian had been focusing more fully on the invitation.

> You are invited to our Grand Opening:
> Our new club caters to everyone, whoever you are. So, come as you are. Come as you want. Come as you need to be. We will not judge. We are here for you.

Brian clicked on the invite and it "unfolded" like a piece of paper on his screen. The new paper gave the VR location and code for the club as well as the times for the grand opening.

Come as you are. Come as you want to be. Brian realized that he could use mods there. This could be his chance. He could go "looking good" and get to know a girl. Once she got to know him, it wouldn't matter how he looked. She would like him for him. What's more, the club was advertising that not everyone would be real world looking. Brian just hoped that since some were, that would keep some of the more bizarre modifications out. It would be hard to meet someone if they were a fish and you didn't even know if they were male or female.

Brian started whistling as he went through the mods he had in order to build and design an avatar. He wanted it to be good looking, but not completely unrealistic. The more he shaped his avatar, the more excited he got. This was it. He would show Chad that he could get girls without him. He would show Alison and Susan. He didn't need them. He would find new girls that did appreciate him.

Once he was done, Brian leaned back in his chair and looked at the avatar on the screen to see if it needed any final tweaks. Once he was done, he would load it all in his VR program. He was using his slimming mod, increasing its capability until it would take 70 pounds off. He had used an athletic mod to give himself muscles. The program did more toning than build muscles. Brian had been tempted to give himself a "six pack", but had wanted to stay at least a little realistic.

He had kept his basic round face shape, but the slimming mod had made it less puffy. He had made his eyebrows less heavy and lightened them up some. He had widened his eyes, so they were both bigger and slightly farther apart. He was really turning into quite the handsome guy. Now if he could just figure out a plan with his hair, he would be done.

Brian played with the hair, finally settling on a two-layer haircut. Short on the sides, longer on top with spikes. The cut made his face look longer and thinner. It also seemed hip and like something Chad would wear. Brian thought it suited his face. His avatar finalized, Brain loaded all the mods and the club programming into his VR set up. He moved over to the couch and slipped into his VR suit. He could now run everything from his goggles by moving his eyes.

Brain found himself outside of what would be called a "dive bar". The club's facade was brick with a big window where you could look in and see everyone inside. Neon signs in the window blinked open along with the club's name - Xanadu. The main door was green and wooden with a huge bouncer standing in front of it. The bouncer was dressed in a suit and tie. He looked like he was retired from the FBI. Black glasses and an earpiece completed his look.

As Brian walked up, he asked him, "Modifications?"

Brian gulped. "I thought they were allowed." He could feel his embarrassment start to rise.

"Yes, we just want to register them before you enter. You will also be given a bracelet based on your modification status."

Brian was unsure what to think about this, but it was too late to back out now. "Yes."

The bouncer produced a wand similar to the one used at Nebula. He waved it over Brian and the light blinked orange. The bouncer produced a glowing, orange bracelet. "You must have this visible at all times while you are in the club. White is zero mods, blue is up to 25%, green to 50%, orange is up to 75% and red means up to 100%, including possible sex change.

"Tampering with them to change their color is expressly forbidden. A first offense will result in being thrown out of the club. A second offense will result in you being banned. Any questions?"

Brian stared at the bouncer, not sure what if anything to say. Slowly, he shook his head 'no'. The bouncer stepped aside opening the door.

Brian stepped into the club. It was not as fancy as Nebula, or as large. One side of the room was made up of the bar and bar stools. Brian found an empty stool and ordered a beer. Receiving his drink, Brian turned around and surveyed the rest of the room.

At the opposite side of the room was a small stage with a "live" band. A small dance floor in front of the stage was crowded with dancers. Between the bar and the dance floor were scattered tables arranged to seat 4-8 people. People moved around the tables going from the dance floor to the bar. Brian could see the glowing bracelets on everyone. He spotted a few reds and oranges. But most people had green or blue. One table of people seemed to be the only whites in the room.

Brian began to wish that he had maybe used a few less mods. He felt like he stuck out with his orange bracelet. As he turned back to the bar, he noticed a young woman sitting a few seats down from him. She appeared to be alone. He could not see her bracelet from this side. He caught her eye and smiled at her. She smiled back shyly.

Brian moved to an empty seat beside her. "Hi, my name is Brian," he started the conversation.

"I'm Ginger," she answered as she brushed her auburn bangs from her faces. Brian caught sight of her wristband and realized that hers was white. He took a sip of his drink and used that as cover to check her out.

Brian observed that Ginger was short and curvy. She was wearing a tight white wrap shirt that clung to her curves and highlighted her golden skin. She had short auburn hair cut in a pixie cut; the haircut setting off her heart shaped face. Large hazel eyes completed her look. Brian realized that since she was wearing white, how she appeared, must be how she looked in real life.

Brian waved the bartender over and bought Ginger and himself another drink. "I wasn't sure what to expect when I got the invite tonight," he said.

Ginger took her drink answering him, "I don't usually go to bars with mods allowed. But I thought I would check this one out. I like the bracelet system."

Brian nodded. "I have never been to a full mod club," he told her, "but I'm like you… I was curious about this place."

Brian and Ginger talked for a while and drank their beers. They shared some stories about different clubs they had been in and their current jobs. As Brian raised his arm to signal the bartender to bring them another round, he realized that Ginger was staring at his bracelet. He moved his arm down to his side and looked embarrassed. "I thought since I was coming, I might as well try out some mods."

Ginger nodded as she looked down at her drink. Brian felt uncomfortable and awkward. He stumbled around in his mind trying to come up with something to say. He was beginning to understand that this was harder than just looking good. Suddenly he blurted out, "I know I shouldn't have used so much, but I'm kind of heavy and I just wanted to look skinny."

Brian instantly averted his gaze as he realized what he said. He felt mortified. "I'm sorry. I will be going," he mumbled as he started to get up.

Ginger reached out placing her hand on his arm. "Wait, stay. I didn't mean to seem like I was judging you. You really should be more confident in how you look."

Brian eased back down on the stool. "I have a friend. He makes talking to women seem so easy. I just never know what to say. I don't know how to look. I just don't make friends so easily. I'm not even sure why I am telling you all this."

Ginger laughed. "Because it is easy to say things to people you think you will never see again."

Brian gulped his drink. "But, will we?"

"Will we what?"

"Never see each other again?" Brian asked.

Ginger turned and captured Brian's gaze staring deeply into his eyes. Brian felt like she was studying his very soul. When she finally spoke, he had to lean forward to hear her. "You seem like a nice guy. In another time and place, I might even like getting to know you. But right now, I don't have time in my life for guys that cannot be confident in themselves.

"Thanks for the drink. Maybe if you ever have more confidence we will meet up and it will be different." With that, she slipped off the stool and eased through the crowd towards the dance floor.

Brian sat following her with his eyes. He was not even sure what had gone wrong. She had seemed to be okay with his orange bracelet and even took his drink. But then she was gone, just like all the rest. It didn't seem to matter what he did. He was never going to get a girl.

Brian slopped beer on the bar as he slammed his drink down. He marched to the portal and keyed in the sequence to leave the bar and VR.

Back in his apartment, Brian sat up and began putting his equipment away. He hovered between anger and tears. He felt so stupid. Of course, someone as perfect as Ginger would not want him once she knew he was an orange and not perfect. How could he be so stupid? He was done. He was not going to any more clubs.

Chapter Thirteen

Brian moved to his computer. As he was logging onto his forum, he again noticed the golden ticket icon sparkling at the bottom of his screen. He hovered the cursor over it, but could not make himself click it. The longer he sat in front of the screen reading the posts of the other guys, the madder and bleaker he got. Brian's resentment continued to grow. He got to the point that he was no longer really reading the posts, but just skimming over them. His real thoughts were on his life.

Brian mentally looked at his life. He had a job that he could not advance in. He had friends, Chad and Susan, that were not really friends. He had a woman he wanted to date who did not want him, Alison. He had this crappy little apartment that basically housed his computer, VR, a place to sleep, and a place to cook.

The only thing Brian really had was his message board and the guys on it. They had been there for him when no one else had been. Yes, some of them took it too far, but maybe it was time to begin to "take things farther." Brian sat staring blankly in front of him as he tried to organize his thoughts. Why did the women get to have all the power? Why did they decide some men were unworthy of sex?

Who were they that they got to keep him an incel. No man should ever have to be an incel.

Brian's anger and humiliation at how he had been treated continued to grow. He knew that if he reached out and posted, the guys would support him, but so what? Tomorrow, he would still be single. Tomorrow, he would still be alone. They were there for him, but they would never really be in his life. And the people that were in his life didn't understand him.

Brian reached for his keyboard and began to type what he thinking. He poured his feelings into developing a creed of not only what his life was, but what he wanted his life to be. Brian injected his pain of rejection and his feelings of betrayal into the statement. All of his loneliness and fear for the future went into it. When Brian was done, he read over what he had written.

Women have been in control of men's lives for too long. They have created two classes of men, those they will date and those they will not date. This creates a subclass of men who have no choice but to remain celibate. They may not want to be, but they are forced to stay this way because of women's refusal to date them.

The other class of men are freely given sex, often by multiple women. The scarcity for some is not due to a lack of women, but by certain men getting more than their own share of women. These men do not know what it is like to go without sex. They do not know the pain of constant rejection. Often if they do know, they do not care.

Women make this distinction of those who will and will not get sex based on how a man looks. They do not care about a guy's personality, or job, or even his ability or willingness to be faithful. They are only looking for someone they find attractive. Then they are on to the next man. Never caring about those they reject.

I say it is time to end this disparity. I say it is time to end this power that women have over men's lives. We need to take back what is ours. We should never have to do without what other men have in overabundance. It is time that women have to treat all men as equal. They should no longer be allowed to have sex with only those that are handsome. All men should have the same right to women.

Brian's manifesto when on for another two pages. But it basically continued to be a play on the same theme. Brian did not want to advocate for violence. So his statement rambled about what he wanted, without saying exactly how it would come to pass. In fact, he wasn't even sure if he meant what he said, or if he was just venting. But he knew he did not want to be alone for the rest of his life.

Brian posted his writings to the board. He knew it would result in several new messages. But he felt emotionally drained after writing it. He put his board on mute, silenced his phone, and headed to bed. As he lay alone in his bed, his thoughts turned to Alison. He wondered if she was with Chad again tonight.

Chapter Fourteen

Brian got up late Sunday morning and sulked in bed. He finally got up when it became apparent that he was not going back to sleep. Brian did a few household chores that he had blown off the day before getting ready to go the club. Looking back, it would have been time better spent doing his chores. He tried to watch a movie, but could not really follow and turned it off when he realized he did not even know the characters on the screen.

Brian continued to avoid his computer. He knew that once he opened the forum, he would be inundated with messages and response posts. With a deep breath, he decided it was time. But when his computer logged on, the golden ticket popped up on the screen, with a message.

MAKE YOUR RESERVATION NOW. THE RED DOOR SALOON HAS A LIMITED NUMBER OF OPENING. CLICK NOW TO MAKE SURE YOU GET YOURS.

Brian looked at the message. "What the hell," he thought, "I might as well give it a try. I'm never going to have sex any other way."

Brian clicked on the message. Several forms popped up for Brian to fill out. The first was a form discussing Brian's health history. The next few forms reviewed the club rules and expectations. One explained the "adult nature" of the "experience" and Brian had to click that he accepted this. He also had to agree to follow the rules, which mostly consisted of not damaging the equipment and not telling anyone anything he saw while in the saloon. The last Brian thought was interesting, but he clicked 'yes'.

The last form was more technical and discussed his VR set up in detail. After he completed it, a list of additional items was generated. At the bottom, the form stated these items were available for loan free of charge due to his VIP status. Brian again clicked 'yes'. At this point several new forms were zapped into existence. Brian hung his head and rubbed his hand across his forehead. He was just about to quit, when he noticed he had received a message from Chad.

The message had been sent early this morning. Brian had just now noticed it. Chad had written telling Brian he was sorry for everything. He had not intended to start up with Alison. But now he really liked her. Chad finished by saying he hoped they could still be friends. Brian clenched his hands into fists and ground his teeth. "Hope they can still be friends". Brian could hear that phrase echoing in his mind from every girl who had ever rejected him.

Brian hit the delete button and went back to the forms. He barely even read them as he quickly scrolled through them clicking okay. He put in his address so the needed items could be shipped to him and accepted responsibility for them if he should damage them. He agreed to return them when finished. In his current state, Brian would have clicked okay to about anything if it would have meant he could get his appointment scheduled.

The final screens were simple. Brian received a tracking number and date of delivery. He was given instructions on how to set a reservation based on when the items were to arrive. Finally, he was able to access the reservations system. Since the extra VR equipment was to arrive by Thursday, he made an appointment for next Saturday night, 7-10 pm.

"It's not like I will have anything else to do at that time," Brian said to himself.

The final set of instructions informed Brian that he would need to have all his equipment up and running by 6:30 so that he would have time to make sure it all worked correctly and to make the final touches to his experience before it started at seven. Brian wasn't sure what that meant, but he clicked accept one last time. Brian sagged in his chair once he had completed it. *What's done is done*, he thought.

Chapter Fifteen

Brian moped through the next week. He went to work, but didn't interact with anyone. Jerry informed him a group was going bowling again. Brian thanked him, but stated he was busy. He was sure that Alison and Chad would be there and he did not want to see that. Susan tried to contact him at work. He deleted the message without reading it and blocked her from contacting him that way. He toyed with the idea of blocking Alison and Chad, but why bother? Other than Chad's one message, they were not reaching out to him.

Brian spent his evenings home alone, mostly on his message board. Many of the members were commenting on his post. Across the board, they all supported the main ideas behind it, but were divided on what to do. The more violent members called for physically forcing women to change. Other members said violence wasn't an answer, but like Brian, had no idea how to change the status quo outside of violence.

One forum member had suggested a lottery system. Each child born was assigned a number at birth and at a specific age they would be randomly paired with the opposite sex. Whoever you were paired with could be your only sex partner. Brian liked the idea in theory. But he knew it would never come to pass. How could you enforce it? How could you set up such a system? As another forum member stated, women also tended to have sex with men in power. They would not want to use their power to create a system that would give up that power to have sex whenever they wanted.

Brian was glad to have the support, but it just reinforced his belief that he was never having sex. No matter what solution was suggested, the only way to implement it meant using violence. Those with looks, money, and power would never support changing things and losing their advantages. By Thursday, Brian was even more depressed than when he had made his reservation.

He had almost forgotten that the extra VR items were coming until he got home from work and found packages on his front porch. He had a moment of panic thinking all his neighbors knew he had gotten a delivery from the sex club. As he looked at the packages more closely, he realized they had no logo and the return label was only a shipping box. No one would be able to tell where they came from. Breathing a sigh of relief, he hauled all the items into apartment.

Brian carefully unpacked the equipment and reviewed the enclosed invoice and instructions. Everything seemed to be accounted for. He was a little unclear on some of the items, but carefully read the directions. As he read, he realized that the additional items were to make his experience "more real". Brian got embarrassed reading how he was supposed to use some of the pieces and put everything aside. He continued to be excited about his upcoming "night out" as he was calling it in his mind, but he also now had some trepidation. How exactly was this going to work?

Brian had thought Saturday would never arrive. Friday at work, he was short and snappy with all his co-workers. He even snapped at Jerry when he stopped at Brian's desk.

"Hey, I just wanted to let you know again about bowling," Jerry said with his big sappy grin. "I know you had to leave early last week, so I hoped you would come this week. Why was it that you had to leave early?"

Brian had pushed his dark hair out of his eyes again as he looked up in Jerry's brown eyes. At first, he thought, Jerry might be trying to poke fun at him because of Chad and Alison, but Jerry's face showed only honest confusion. He continued, "I thought you were having fun."

"I just got to feeling bad, Jerry," Brian answered. "Nothing important."

Jerry clapped Brian on the shoulder. He gained back his smile. "I told you the other day, you have to watch out for low blood sugar. Too much junk food."

Brian nodded. "I know Jerry, I know."

"So make sure you eat good before you come this time," Jerry said.

Brian could feel his temper rising. He tried to clamp it down. But he was short and snappy, "I told you I was not coming."

Jerry's face fell. He took a step back as if he had taken a body blow. "I was just being nice," Jerry stated. "I thought you liked me."

Brian felt horrible as he watched Jerry turn away. He hitched up his pants as he started his retreat towards his desk in the front of the office. Brian started to call out to him, but stopped himself. What would he say? "Yeah, Jerry I do like you. But you see Alison was supposed to be my date and now she's screwing Chad. So no, I really don't want to go bowling and see them having fun."

He would make it up to Jerry later. When he went to lunch, he would stop by the bakery Jerry liked and get some of his favorite cookies. He just hoped Jerry would not mention bowling or Alison to him again.

When Saturday finally arrived, Brian was so keyed up, he had woken up at 5:30 am. He tried on his VR suit three times before noon and re-read all his instructions four times. He tried to keep his mind off the "upcoming event", but his eyes kept going back to his VR couch and the equipment laid out on it. He logged into his forum, but he couldn't keep his mind on the topics and posts. He tried cleaning, but had very few chores to do and they did not distract him. He even tried watching TV and had no luck with that either.

Brian eventually decided to take a shower. He knew that it wouldn't really matter in VR, but he wanted to be careful with the VR items. The instructions had stated if they were returned damaged or dirty, he would have to pay a cleaning or repair fee. Brian did not want to think about that. Whatever it cost, he was sure his VIP pass would not cover it.

Brian found the hot water and routine of the shower to be soothing. When he was finished, he shaved. Staring in the mirror, he inspected his dark hair as it hung limply around his face. He remembered the stylish cut he had used at Xanadu. Why couldn't he just have his hair cut like that. He had really liked the look. It made his face seem less moon-like, and he had seemed stylish. Brian stood there as the steam covered the mirror imagining what he would look like every day with that hair style. When the steam became too thick, he wiped it with his towel and wiped away his fantasies as he was confronted with his pale, pasty, moon face with his dark sunken eyes and straight hair clinging to the wetness on the edges. This was his reality.

Brian carefully dried off. He knew from the instructions, he needed to make sure he was not wet when putting on his suit. It could interfere with the interface and he would not have a good connection. That would make the experience less intense. Brian stood in front of his bedroom fan, naked, turning this way and that as the fan blew on him. He knew he was probably being overly cautious. But he may never get another experience like this. He wanted to make the best of it.

Once Brian was sure that he was completely dry, he slowly began putting on his VR suit. The suit looked like giant footed pajamas with gloves. The gloves could be folded back to allow his hands to emerge from the wrists of the suit. He would put the gloves on once the program was running. The program would then sense the movements of his fingers within the gloves and use that as input rather than his keyboard.

The suit was made out of some flexible silicone like material. It reminded Brian vaguely of a wet suit, but once it was on, it was warm and moved easily with his body. If he didn't see it on his body, he would almost think he was still standing naked in the room it was so light-weight and free.

Brian had just slid it on the times he had tried it on in the past. But now, he slowly put his first foot in, making sure that each sensor was making contact with his skin. The suit had hundreds of little pads that needed to be in direct contact with his skin. These pads would sense his movement so his avatar would more completely mimic his movements than Brian had ever experienced. They would also send signals to the suit and through the suit to Brian to mimic the feel of what his avatar was experiencing.

The directions had stated that the suit was designed to ensure contact on its own, but Brian felt reassured trying to touch each one as he slipped on first one leg and then the other into the suit. He knew that he would not be able to do this with his back, but it comforted him. It gave him something to focus on so he was not so nervous about the upcoming "event."

Once Brian had the suit to his waist, he needed to attach the portion that went over his private parts. Brian stood looking in the mirror, embarrassed. He wondered if he could just leave this part out. But the instructions had been quite clear. If he did not, he risked having a bad experience and also damaging the suit. Standing there, holding the cup like receptacle in one hand and holding the suit open in his other, Brian felt ridiculous standing in front of the mirror. His stomach protruded out slightly in his way.

Brian stood several minutes looking in the mirror. He decided he might as well get this over with. He reached down with his one hand as he used his other hand to hold everything back and slowly, he nestled the cup into his suit so that it was resting over himself. He pressed firmly so that the cup and suit made a good connection and then pulled the suit up and tight against his body. Brian could feel the receptacle slide into place as the instructions said it would. It felt so soft and smooth against him, Brian could already feel a slight electric tingle growing.

This had been the most embarrassing part of the instructions as they explained how this would happen, but he was just supposed to ignore it and continue dressing. They stated it would fade until later during the program. Brian felt his face flush. How could anyone ignore this? He tried to resume dressing, but the tingle was distracting. Finally, he took some deep breaths, concentrated on his suit and made sure his arms were in correctly and connected.

When he was done, Brian checked the time. It was only 6 pm. He moved from his bedroom to the living room, the suit slightly caressing him as he moved. Brian had not experienced this in the past as he had taken it off right after putting it on. He could feel an anticipation building as the suit continued to move against his skin. It reminded him of when you could feel electricity in the air during a building thunderstorm. But this was playing up and down his skin.

Brian got the final piece of his suit that he had left near his computer. A thin hood that enclosed the front and back of his head. The first time he had tried it on, it had felt almost claustrophobic to him. But after taking it on and off a few times, Brian could tolerate it. He hoped that once he was immersed in VR, it would not bother him as much. He only had goggles and had never worn a full immersion hood. He knew it would take some getting used to.

Putting the hood into place and pressing, he could feel the connections snap into place. All that was left was to start the program and move to his couch. Brian knew he was early, but he hoped he would be able to at least get started. He did not think he wanted to wait much longer. So he went to his computer and clicked the ticket. He then loaded the program from the computer to his VR system. He connected his suit to his VR system and was suddenly hit with another even more intense layer of sensation.

Brian carefully walked to his couch. Pulling the gloves over his hands, his fingers twitched to get the program open. He then hit the enter key. Suddenly he was plunged into total darkness, except a small circle of golden light he was standing in. In front of him was a woman dressed like an Old West can-can girl. She had mocha colored skin, dark brown eyes, and her dark curly hair was piled on her head. Her black dress was offset with bright red. It fell tightly from her shoulders to her waist, where her full skirt spread out around her.

Chapter Sixteen

"I'm Athena. I am to be your guide tonight," she spoke in crisp English, sounding almost faintly British. "If you would like, you can adjust my appearance more to your liking."

"N-n-no," Brian uttered, "you are fine."

Athena tipped her head forward in a short, quick nod. "It is my job to make sure you have connected your suit correctly, go over the final consents, and then help you create your partner and storyline."

"M-m-my story line?" Brian questioned.

"We like to make sure that every person's experience at the Red Door Saloon is tailored to their wants and needs. We add elements to our characters and setting to ensure this happens. Don't worry, we will cover that," Athena answered. "But first we need to test your suit."

Athena took Brain through a series of exercises. She had him move various parts of his body and sent signals though his contacts to make sure they were all working. The experience was so realistic that at the end Brian felt as if he had been exercising and was almost out of breath. Athena checked a tablet that had suddenly appeared in her hands. "It looks like everything is in proper working order."

"Now it's time to begin to set up your experience," Athena stated as she created several different screens. "We have a selection of basic packages that can be customized. You have full control over the creation of both your construct and your storyline with your VIP pass."

On the different screen, Brian could see various potential options. As he looked at each, Brian found himself getting more and more uncertain about this. Many of the screens showed things he had never even known existed, let alone wanted to try. He could feel himself getting overwhelmed and he began to blush.

Athena sensed his discomfort and with a wave of her hands, she waved everything away. "Let's start smaller, shall we?" She again pulled the tablet out of the air. "Let's start with the basics and go from there."

Athena consulted her tablet. "You have to pick the sex of your partner."

Brian looked at Athena dumbfounded. What did she mean? He didn't want to admit that he didn't know, but he also was not sure what she was talking about.

Athena looked up from her tablet when she noticed that Brian was not answering her. "Do you want to have sex with a man or a woman? "

Brian blushed. Then he realized that Athena would know he was blushing this VR was so realistic and blushed even more. "A w-w-woman."

Athena nodded and clicked a box on her tablet. "Would you like to design her or just pick from one of our types?"

Brian again wasn't sure what to say. He stared blankly at Athena. "I w-w-would like to p-p-pick her out."

Athena nodded and clicked a box. The screens popped into existence again, each one showing another girl. They were all beautiful and dressed in different variations of Athena's outfit. Some were different colors. Others revealed more. Brian's head slowly swiveled from screen to screen trying to take it in.

His eyes landed on one girl. She was dressed in a black outfit with purple trimmings. Her neckline plunged between her two breasts. Her skirt was sheer black showing purple spank type shorts underneath that barely covered anything. The side of the screen showed her height to be on the short side. She looked fit, without being overly muscular. On the screen she moved with grace. She had chestnut hair that was pulled up into a ponytail and then fell from her crown to just below her shoulders. Her oval face contained two large hazel eyes that were enhanced by her high cheekbones. But what really caught Brian's attention was her smile. It made her whole face light up.

Brian pointed to the screen. "I want this one."

Athena again waved her hands and all the other screens disappeared. "Do you want to make any changes?"

Brian considered it carefully. "Can we make her nose smaller? More pert? Just barely."

Athena made some adjustments until Brian said, "There. Yes, just like that. Now can you keep the hair color, but make it a different style? I want it to be perfectly straight. It should swing around her face when she moves, but not go much below her shoulders."

Athena again made the corrections. Brian watched as the image on the screen became closer and closer to the girl he was imagining. As Athena was making the last adjustment, Brian glanced away. When Athena announced, "It's done." He looked back at the screen. Brian gaped.

He had not been doing it on purpose, but he had been designing Alison. His ideal woman was still her. He started to tell Athena to change it. But then he stopped himself. Why should he? The more he thought about it the more he wanted this version. Alison would never know. What would be the harm?

Brian nodded. "That is perfect."

Athena stated, "We need to make your storyline. We have everything here. Damsel in distress, simple, complex, S&M, anything goes."

Brian found himself flushing from embarrassment again. "I just want something simple. I just want...." he trailed off not sure what he wanted or expected. He could feel himself getting more and more upset and frustrated. Even when it was a sure thing it was almost too complicated for him to handle.

Athena stated, "We have a pretty basic simple package. The storyline is about a dad taking his son for sex for the first time. I could do a few tweaks and it would be perfect for you. Is this your first time?"

Brian looked aghast at the avatar. She seemed to really understand and catch the nuances of his body language. Way more than an AI computer program should. Brian began to wonder if this was an actual person in VR with him. He thought back to all the pages and pages of information and how he had flown through it at the end. He couldn't remember what it had said about his guide. He got so flustered thinking that Athena might be an actual person he didn't realize she was waiting on him.

Brian looks up briefly making eye contact with her. Athena asked again, "Is this your first time?"

Brian nodded, too embarrassed to speak. Athena checked another box. She then turned her tablet towards Brian. "Here are all the last few questions and consents. Please take your time reading through them and when you are satisfied with your answers hit accept."

Brian mutely took the tablet and started to read the forms. Embarrassed and just wanting this over, he stopped reading after the first paragraph. He just started clicking okay to every question.

Do you consent to having close personal contact? Okay

Do you acknowledge that if you have health problems this could be dangerous? Okay

Do you consent to having this avatar and storyline? Okay

Do you consent to full body immersion VR? Okay

Brian continued clicking 'okay', not even reading any of the rest of them. When he was done, Athena took back the tablet and reviewed his answers. Brian saw her raise her eyebrows at some of his answers, but he didn't have it in him to try and double check them. He was already beginning to regret coming. He thought about Chad. How had Chad known about a place like this? Would he ever use a place like this? Brian shook his head. He didn't really want to know any of those answers. But he could guess that Chad would have been way smoother about this whole process.

Athena tapped something on the tablet and then looked at Brian. "It is ready. Just close your eyes. Count slowly backwards from 20. When you open your eyes, you will be there. I hope you enjoy your trip." With that she disappeared.

Brian closed his eyes and counted.

Chapter Seventeen

When Brian opened his eyes, it was as if he were standing in a movie. He was on the edge of a Western town. The street appeared to be about two blocks long. On one side, there was a general store, a doctor's office, and some other business, ending with a stable at the other end. Brian found himself standing in front of the jail on his side of the street. He could see a bank and the saloon on down the sidewalk. The streets were full of people on horseback and others were walking on the sidewalks.

Brian slowly looked around trying to get his bearings. Were all these people VR? Were the other people in the program right now? The "people" looked so real. Brian found it hard to believe that they were all avatars. But why would they be here? As he continued to gawk, a man bumped into him and almost knocked him off his feet. "Get out of my way. I don't have time to just stand here," the man stated as he hurried away.

Brian turned to watch the man, then turned back towards the saloon. It had the traditional double swinging wooden doors painted a bright red color. He could see various men and women through the window. As he was looking, he caught sight of the character he had developed. She was on stage dancing. As she flounced her skirt doing the can-can, he could catch glimpses of what was underneath through the sheer material. Her hair flowed around her face. Brian was captivated by her smile.

Without even knowing he was doing it, he walked to the saloon and pushed through the entrance. He moved to the bar, never taking his eyes of the girl. As he pulled up a bar stool, the bartender noticed where he was looking. "That's Rose. She is real popular with the customers."

Brian accepted the beer sat in front of him and continued to watch. Twice, Rose appeared to make eye contact with him. "When is she done dancing?" he asked the bartender.

"This is her last song," the bartender answered.

When the song was over, Brian watched Rose approach. "Can I buy you a beer?" he asked.

Rose reached down and took his beer, never breaking eye contact, and took a swig of it. Then carefully licked the foam off her pink rosebud mouth. "I'm just fine sharing if you are," she replied. Rose then pulled her bar stool close enough that when she sat down, Brian could not help but brush up against her to reach his glass. As he did, Rose leaned into him and put her hand on his thigh.

Brian gulped his beer and could feel it all the way down. This experience was so real he just couldn't believe it. Brian tried to think of something to say, but his mind was blank. He just looked at Rose, not knowing what to do or say. "N-n-nice to meet you," he finally stammered.

Rose got a sweet smile. "You don't have to be so nervous around me. I'm here for you," she stated and then leaned in and gave Brian a small kiss on the cheek.

"B-b-but, don't you have any say in this?" Brian asked. Then he instantly felt stupid. Rose was just a computer construct. A piece of VR code. Of course, she didn't have any say in this matter. What was he thinking? But the experience seemed so real, he found himself getting caught up in the moment.

Rose did not seem to think he was stupid. Her smile widened and brightened. "Aren't you just the sweetest thing," she cooed as she caressed his thigh with her hand as she draped her other arm on the bar, leaning even farther forward. "I could just eat you up."

Brian was beginning to feel hot and flushed, but not with embarrassment. He was keenly aware of Rose's hand on his leg and his cheek still tingled from her kiss. He felt comfort in her smile. Leaning over he cupped her face and gave her a soft kiss on the lips. He could smell her perfume and sweat from dancing and her lips tasted so sweet. Brian drew in a deep breath as he felt a clenching in his groin.

Rose smiled and gave a small giggle. She reached for the beer glass and took another sip. Again licking the foam from her lips. "I don't think I have ever seen you here before," she stated.

Brian pushed his glass toward the bartender and nodded for him to pour another one. Getting into the role, he nodded. "I just rode into town today. I'm looking for some relaxation for the evening."

Rose giggled. She reached over and with her delicate, soft fingers outlined his lips. She traced her finger down his throat until it reached the top of his shirt collar. "Well, I wonder what we could find for you to do in this boring town," she purred.

Brian reached for his new beer and took another gulp as he felt a fire deep in his belly. He could feel a tightening in his groin that only seemed to pull tighter each time Rose touched him. Brian reached out and touched her hair. It was like touching silk. He loved how it slithered through his hands.

Rose pulled back, catching his hand. "Let's go somewhere more comfortable where we can get to know each other," she spoke quietly.

Brian let Rose pull him towards the side of the stage where he had not noticed a door. Rose waved her hand in front of it allowing it to open. Brian came to a halt when he walked through the door. The room appeared to be like a luxurious sitting room in an old Victorian style house. Overly stuffed chairs, couches and pillows were scattered all over the room. Women of different stages of undress lounged on the furniture. A few men were in the room.

Brian felt Rose tug on his hand as she pulled him over to a corner. There she sat on a couch and pulled him down beside her.

"Let's get to know each other better," she breathed into his ear as she leaned in close.

Brian pulled back slightly, overwhelmed by how fast things were going. "Wh-wh-what would you like to know about me?" he asked.

Rose took her hands and gave him feather light touches on his face, chest, arm, and thigh, saying with each touch, "Do you like to be touched here?"

Brian felt heat bloom at each spot and electric fire flashed from her touch and down his skin. He leaned forwarded and breathed in her scent, feeling a peace and calm roll over him, while at the same time on another level a tension was building.

Rose giggled and flashed that sparkling smile as the kiss ended. She leaned forward and ran both her hands up his thighs leaning forward so her lips were almost touching his mouth. "I want to know what you want."

Brian swallowed nervously. "I th-th-think I would like to take it slow. I'm just a little-. I don't know-. I just…" Brian trailed off as Rose put her finger on his lips. She gently traced him mouth maintaining eye contact with him the whole time.

"It's okay. You don't have to be nervous. We can just sit here and have some fun for a while first. We are in no hurry," Rose commented as she continued to trace patterns with her finger over his lips and down Brian's chest. "You just need to relax."

Brian slowly ran his finger along Rose's jawline, down her neck and across her shoulders. Her skin was as creamy soft as it looked. He ached to run his hands all over her body. Reaching out he entwined his arms around her and pulled her close. Bending down, he crushed her velvety lips with his deep kiss tasting her mouth.

Brian shuddered slightly as the kiss ended. Pulling back, he gazed into Rose's eyes. He felt himself wanting to melt into their hazel color. The more he focused on them, the more the colors changed and flashed, first blue, then green, then brown, then back. Brian found himself getting lost in Rose's eyes.

Rose never broke eye contact as she slowly reached in and kissed Brian again. She started soft and slow, but gradually built up pressure until Brian started to respond. He tightened his arms around her and pulled her to him tight. As he could feel tension start to build within him, his kisses grew more frantic. He kissed her deeply, until it was like he was trying to consume her mouth with his. The whole time, Rose continued to caress his back and thighs. Brian felt as if the very skin where she was touching was on fire. He had never experienced sensations so real while he was in VR. He tried to tell himself it wasn't real, but it felt so good.

Rose withdrew slightly and smiled. "Isn't that better?"

Brian smiled and pulled her back in. "Yes," he answered as he resumed kissing her. As Brian got more excited, his hands started to roam. He pushed them up and under Rose's top and cupped her breasts. He shuddered as he could feel Rose's hands move closer to his crotch. The sound of another woman laughing pulled him out of it.

Brian pulled back from Rose and looked around the room. He could see couples in various corners. The dim lighting and the layout of the furniture and walls made it hard to tell exactly what was happening. But from the sighs and rustling of clothes, Brian had a pretty good idea of what was going on. Embarrassment flooded him as he realized how far he had taken things where anyone could see. Breathing heavily, he stated, "Not here."

Rose stood and led Brian up the stairs to a small bedroom. It was furnished with a small dressing table and mirror with a bench for sitting. The only other item in the room was a huge replica of a queen-sized feather bed. Brian sunk down into the opulent softness as he sat on the edge of the bed. He caught the string that laced up the front of Rose's top with one hand and pulled. The top pulled open and fell to the ground.

Brian drank in the sight of her breasts and reached to cup them. Hesitant, he pulled back unsure of what to do. Rose reached for his hands stroking them as she placed them on her breasts. Brian sighed as he felt the weight of them in his hands. He could fell himself hardening and he ached with need. Rose gently ran her hands up and down her arms almost as if she were coaching his hand move-ments. He slowly lowered his mouth and groaned with delight as he took her in his mouth.

Rose reached out and began to draw Brian's shirt up his back and over his head. Brian moved with her to help accomplish getting his shirt off and then buried his face back into her breasts. Rose began to grip his arms tightly as she arched her back in delight. Brian was surprised and distracted as he noticed that she was beginning to moan with her pleasure. The sounds caused him to flush and added to his own pleasure. He had never expected this experience to be so intense and so real down to even having the construct mimic a sexual response.

Rose grasped Brian's chin and pulled his head to get back his attention. She leaned down and kissed him deeply holding his face in her hands. As she pulled back to break the kiss, she placed her hands on her hips and pushed her skirt to the floor. Standing completely nude in front of Brian she leaned back into him and kissed him again. Brian found his hands roaming over her body as his own arousal grew.

"Silly boy, you have too many clothes on," Rose teased. Rose moved to undo his jeans. Brian remembered that he had no mods here and felt ashamed about his stomach and body. He tried to pull back.

"No, that's okay. Why don't we turn out the light?" he stated feeling awkward.

Rose shook her head and reached for his pants again. "No, you don't have to worry. I can't wait to see your body." Rose pushed him back on the bed and began to pull his jeans down.

Brian closed his eyes as Rose pulled them off waiting for her comment. When one did not come, he looked up slightly through narrowed eyelids. Rose put one perfectly manicured finger under his chin and raised his face to meet her eyes. Then she leaned down and kissed him pushing him back on the bed. As Brian started to rise, Rose reached for him and cupped his groin as she lay beside him on the bed smiling at him. "I told you to just relax. It will all be okay," she purred into his ear. Brian melted into her as he felt fire flush through his body from his center outwards.

Brian fumbled his way through his first experience. He felt awkward and strange several times. But Rose was there to calm him and encourage him. By the time he finished, Brian was almost relieved it was over. As he lay on the bed holding Rose in his arms, he wondered how he would ever have been able to get through this in the real world where women expected men to know what they were doing. He had enjoyed it, but it had been stressful. He couldn't imagine doing this with a real live girl in the real world. Maybe it would be better the next time.

Brian could feel Rose lightly running her fingers over his body. Caressing his arms, back, and thighs she made patterns and stroked him. Lightly at first with building pressure. Brian could feel the intensity of her touch building and the electric tingles along his skin with it. He looked at Rose and raised an eyebrow.

Rose smiled as she pulled him in for a kiss. "You have more time left. I hear it is always better after you have had some practice."

Brian smiled and moved towards her. He hoped this time would be better.

Chapter Eighteen

Brian fell asleep lying in Rose's arms. The VR system sensed he was asleep and that his time was gone. The system disengaged the program. Brian woke up as he came out of VR. He looked around his dismal room comparing it to the VR experience he had just had. He felt let down and slightly disgusted with himself. He knew that Rose was not a real girl, but he had used her just as Chad used all the girls he went with. And for what? The second time had been better, but still not great. He had felt awkward and nervous that time also. He had not been able to shut his brain off and just enjoy it. Maybe he should just be an incel. He really didn't seem to know how to interact with girls, not even one that wasn't real.

Brian stripped off the suit and jumped into a shower. He just wanted to wash the whole experience off his body and out of his mind. Chad was right. He had been obsessed about sex. Well, now he had it and he wasn't sure he even really cared.

After he got out of the shower, Brian boxed up the VR equipment he had been sent. The directions had stated that he was allowed to keep it for a period of time in case he wanted to go back. Once it was all boxed up, he put it in the closet. He doubted he would ever use it, but at least he would have it if he needed it again. He really just wanted to forget about it.

Brian went through the next days and weeks in a fog. He went to work. Avoided Alison when he could. He still dodged Chad's phone calls. Susan was still blocked. Some days he felt as if he were being unfair to Susan since he had not blocked Chad and Alison, but he didn't change anything. Whenever he had to get in his closet, he would look at the boxes and slam the door shut. He knew he would never use them, but couldn't quite make himself send the rest back.

When Brian wasn't at work, he was often online. He had started trolling women, making nasty comments and replies to things they posted on social media. He would deliberately pick a fight and then blame the woman. The rest of his time he was on the message board. The group had been building on Brian's manifesto to create a "perfect world" where there would never be another incel. The group was planning how it would be enforced, laws, rules, and even traditions that could be passed from father to son. Brian joined in at times. Mostly, he just sat and read the growing thread. He knew it was all fantasy, but it was nice to dream.

Brian went weeks with no "live" contact with other people outside of work. Out of habit, he answered his phone one evening without thinking or seeing who was calling.

"Brian?"

"Yeah," Brian answered, "who is this?"

"It's me. Chad," came the answer after a brief pause. "I wasn't sure if you would answer. I have tried to call you several times."

Brian let out a breath he had not even realized he was holding. On some level, he had known it was Chad the moment he heard his voice. "So, what do you want?" Brian asked.

Chad hesitated. "I just wanted to, you know, talk."

"Well, then talk," Brian stated.

"You don't have to be so short," complained Chad.

Brian took a deep breath. "Listen, Chad, you called me. We haven't talked in weeks. You stole the girl you knew I wanted to date. I'm not sure what you want from me, but I don't have a lot of patience. In fact, I'm not sure why I answered the phone."

"Don't hang up!" Chad pleaded. "I … Well, I…. I need to tell you I'm sorry."

Brian waited. He was not going to let Chad off the hook that easily. In fact, he highly doubted that Chad was sorry at all. When it became clear Chad was not going to say any more, Brian commented, "Go on."

"I shouldn't have gone out with Alison. That wasn't nice to you. I knew that whole evening was your attempt to date her. I was not a good friend."

"And?" Brian prompted.

"And I screwed up. And I'm sorry. And I would really like to be friends again," Chad stated.

Brian continued to sit in silence. Over the phone, he could not tell if Chad meant it. He almost wished they were screening. But he had been binge eating over the last few weeks since the sex club. He had probably gained about 10 pounds. He didn't know if Chad would be able to tell, but he sure didn't want him to see.

"Brian, are you still there?" Chad interrupted his thoughts.

"Yes."

"Well then say something." Chad's growing frustration was evident.

Brian hid a gleeful smile, "What exactly would you like me to say? No problem that my best friend screwed me over?"

Chad raised his voice, "I apologized. What more do you want? Do you want me to break up with Alison? Do you want me to beg? I don't know why you can't just understand, I NEVER MEANT TO HURT YOU."

Brian thought about one more snide comment, but didn't say it. He was already feeling emotionally exhausted by this conversation. He commented, "I understand. It doesn't make it any better."

Chad blew out a deep breath and spoke quieter, "You know you can really be a shit."

Brian smiled. "Not any worse than you."

"I guess that is right."

Brian said, "I don't really want you to break up, but I kind of do. Not really. I just am still mad."

Chad answered, "Not to be mean, but you know that even if we did break up, she probably wouldn't date you."

Brian shook his head. There was the old Chad he knew. In his attempt to try and rally Brian, all he had done was make things worse. Brian had already figured it out that Alison was unlikely to date him, even without Chad in the picture, but that didn't mean he had to have it rubbed in his face.

Brian asked Chad, "So what do you want?"

"I thought maybe we could hang out again sometime. You know go to the clubs."

Brian shook his head then caught himself. He hit the video button and Chad's face popped up on his screen. "I don't really go to the clubs anymore."

"So what do you do? We could still hang?"

Brian thought about his message boards and his trolling. He couldn't see Chad doing either with him. In fact, he was faintly ashamed to even tell Chad. He knew he should have more in his life, but right now, this was it. "Nothing much. I'm just here most night."

Chad and Brian bantered back and forth for a while longer. Chad suggested various outings and Brian said no. Chad finally got Brian to agree to going to dinner one night.

"But only if it's all guys. No girls. No Alison." Brian was adamant.

Chad shook his head. "You know she really does like you as a friend. She is as upset by this as you are."

Brian highly doubted that. She had lost a friend she barely inter-acted with. He had lost a chance at her. He shook his head. "No."

Chad agreed. They set a date and time. Brian sat there thinking about the phone call. He wondered if Chad had been sincere. Regardless, he needed to get out. This would give him something to do.

Over the next few months, Chad and Brian had dinner at least once every two weeks. They never discussed Alison and she never came. The chatted on the phone now and again. They were able to be friendly, but distant. When one whole section of Chad's life,

Alison, was a forbidden topic, their relationship could never be close.

Brian remembered some of the good things about his friend, but he continued to wait. He kept feeling as if something was going to happen. The more time he spent with Chad, the more he felt he was rushing towards some uncertain future. He kept thinking that Chad was going to spring something on him. Show his true reason for getting back in touch with him. When the impending crisis did hit, it was from a direction that Brian never saw coming.

Chapter Nineteen

Brian woke up early one Saturday morning. The sun was shining. He had a new commitment to getting healthy and was going walking. He promised himself he would go before he even got on his computer. However, over breakfast, he promised himself he would go as soon as he checked his messages. The moment he turned his computer on an alert came across the screen. The top two inches flashed red with black capital letters tracking across.

ATTENTION! ATTENTION! IT IS TIME FOR YOU TO RETURN OUR EQUIPMENT AND TAKE DELIVERY OF YOUR PRODUCT.

Brian looked at the words as they scrolled across the top of his screen over and over. What in the world. What was he supposed to return? What was he supposed to take delivery of? This all may no sense.

As he watched, he noticed that after the final word, there was a symbol. Careful attention showed it to be a pair of swinging saloon doors. Brian looked towards his closet. The sex club was wanting their equipment back. He let out a sigh. That was easy enough. He clicked on the ticker and instantly a directions sheet and shipping forms appeared. Brian carefully went through the forms and printed the labels. He acknowledged that he was sending the items back and that they were not damaged. When he was done, he set a date for "delivery". Brian had no idea what they might be delivering, but he hoped they were as discrete as before.

Putting the questions out of his mind, Brian tidied up his breakfast mess, and got the boxes out of the closet. He affixed the labels and placed them by the door for shipping. After all of that, he decided he had done enough exercise and he did not need to go out for walk. He sat down and got back on his message boards. He also opened several social media sites to begin trolling. By later that day, he had completely forgotten any mysterious delivery and was immersed in his online world.

—————

Brian had almost forgotten about the pick-up when he heard his doorbell ring a few days later. He closed up his computer and went to answer the door. Standing on his porch was a gentleman dressed all in the black. He was wearing black slacks, a back button-down shirt, and a black jacket. On this jacket, he had a discrete logo where a name tag would normally go, just two red wooden hanging saloon style doors. "Mr. Jennings?" he asked.

Brian stood there just looking at the man. It took him a moment or two before he realized what the man had said. "Yes, that's me," he finally answered.

"I have a pick-up and a drop off."

"What?" Brian asked.

The man consulted his clipboard. "It says I have a pick-up and a drop off for you. Mr. Jennings. A Brian Jennings."

Brian answered, "That's me, but I don't understand. I have the boxes for you here right inside the door. But there is nothing to drop off."

The man looked at his clipboard again. "That is not what it says here."

Brian shrugged. He didn't know what could be going on. "Okay, fine whatever. Let's get these boxes out of here first."

The man helped Brian get them through the door. He carried them to a panel truck with a "We Deliver" logo on the side. Brian waited to see what the man thought he would be dropping off. Brian watched as he went around to the back, opened the doors, and loaded the boxes. He made a check on his clip board after each box. He then went around to the other side and got in the side door. Brian could not see what he was doing. When the man moved around the front of the truck, it appeared he was carrying a basket.

Brian grew more and more confused. What could this be? When the man started up the steps to the porch, Brian got a better look at what the man was carrying. He began to break out in a sweat and turned white as a sheet. "What is that?" he demanded.

The man sat the car seat on the porch and extended the clipboard to Brian. "This is your baby created during your experience. Sign here to state you received your delivery."

Brian backed slowly into the house, his hands held up in front of him. "No, no, no, no," he repeated. "It was VR. You can't get pregnant in VR. No. I don't know what kind of joke this is. But take it back."

The man did not even seem to register Brian's words. He scooped up the baby and the car seat then followed Brian in the house. "We guarantee the full body experience. We take making your VR experience as real as possible quite seriously. You asked for the pregnancy option. This is the outcome."

Brian backed across the room until his knees hit his chair forcing him to sit. "I have no idea what you are talking about. I didn't ask for any pregnancy option. And I sure as hell didn't ask for any child. Take it back. I do not accept. Take it back," Brian stated, his voice getting louder with every word.

The man did not even blink. He pulled out a screen. With a few taps, he called up video. "This is you, is it not?"

Brian watched a video of him with Athena. She was in the middle of discussing all of his sexual options. Brian remember how embarrassed and frustrated he was during the whole process. He watched as he clicked okay down the list to every item. The screen froze and enlarged, focusing in on the question he had just clicked 'yes' to.

Do you want a possible pregnancy option from your encounter?

Brian could not take his eyes off the screen. That was him clicking 'okay', but he knew he had not even read the question at the time. Besides how could he even have conceived a child in VR. It was impossible. His mind was in a whirl as he remembered the morning after.

"But I didn't mean it. I didn't really read it. I don't want it. You cannot make me keep it," he pleaded.

The man put the screen away and looked directly at Brian. His face appeared to be chiseled out of stone. His eyes were hard and flint like. His square jaw looked like it could crush rocks. His frown thinned his lips even further. When he spoke, he used short clipped words.

"It does not matter what you read or didn't read. The truth is you were given options and you clicked okay. A child has been created. It is now your legal responsibility to care for her. It is not the child's fault you did not read what you were agreeing to. And by the way, she is a she, not an it."

Brian looked aghast at him. This could not get any worse. Not just a baby, but a girl baby. How would he even care for her? "No, no, no, no," he repeated again. "I have no experience with children. I can't even get a girl that's not a VR construct. I have no business raising a girl child. Just no. Take her back."

The man's face got even harder if that was possible. His voice deepened and came out sounding like gravel through a rock crusher. "Are you telling me you are refusing to accept delivery?" he asked.

He gave a silent stare as he paused. Just when Brian was about to answer, he continued, "Because if so, I will have to report you to the company for child abandonment. They will have to report you to the police."

Brian slowly deflated under his withering gaze. He hung his head. "But, but, but-" he tried to interject."

The man continued as if Brian had never spoken, "Do you know what it is like in jail?"

Brian shook his head.

"You are put in a suit like ours with IV hook ups that feed you. You are then put in a VR prison. No visitors, no outdoor privileges, no watching TV. Just day after day sitting in a cell staring at walls. They say it drives most people crazy in a short time."

Brian knew that it was over. He had heard worst things about prisons. One of the message boards he was on talked about a new tech that was more extreme than VR. Your brain and what made you YOU got downloaded into the VR prison program and then your body was put on ice until you were taken out. Brian didn't want to go to VR prison, but he also definitely didn't want to be experimented on.

"But I really don't even understand how. I was in VR. How do I know she is really mine?" Brian made a last ditch effort.

The man sighed. "That is technical stuff out of my pay grade. It has to do with 3D printing and synthetic material. If you want to know the complete tech, the company can provide you with all that information. If you want a DNA test that can be arranged, but you have to take custody while you wait."

Brian weakly got up. He walked over to the car seat and looked at it. *No, a girl,* he reminded himself. *Not it.* He was the father of a little baby girl. He turned and nodded his head. "I accept delivery. Where do I sign?"

The man, who still had never given Brian his name, pulled out his clipboard. "By signing you are agreeing to take full legal and physical custody of the baby girl. You will care for her and make sure she has everything she needs."

Brian nodded and signed.

"You will also have some forms that will show up in your inbox."

"Of course, I will. Forms is what got me into this mess. Did anyone ever tell your company you have too many forms?"

The man's glacial look returned. Brian tried to meet his gaze and failed, dropping his eyes. "Fine. I will have forms to fill out. What else?"

"The main form will help you register her birth. You will have to give her a name. That one will need to be done as soon as possible. The rest can wait and be READ CAREFULLY so that you can fill them out CORRECTLY. You will also get a list of recommended items that you will need to purchase. We know this is all new and unexpected. So we have tried to prepare a list and some instructions that will help you transition to fatherhood. I would suggest that you also read them FULLY."

Brian swallowed the lump in his throat at the man's words. He knew he had screwed up by not reading the forms completely, but to now have a baby girl. This just seemed ridiculous. But he was not going to risk jail. "I understand," he told the man.

The man started to leave. When he reached the door, he turned back. "One more thing. I have to notify the company that you had to be forced to accept delivery. We will be watching you to ensure this baby is well cared for." With that, he walked out pulling the door shut hard behind himself.

Brian sagged back into the chair. How had this even happened? He had been in VR. This was not supposed to be possible. Nothing made sense to him. But as he watched the baby sleeping in the car seat, he understood it no longer matter how, what matter was what was he doing to do now?

Chapter Twenty

Brian lost track of time as he sat watching the baby sleep. His thoughts continued to whirl. He was in no way prepared to care for a baby. He didn't have any supplies. No daycare. He didn't even know how or where to start. The longer he sat there, the more convinced he became that he needed help. He picked up the phone and started to call Susan. Suddenly, he remembered that he had blocked her and not talked to her in months. *Alison*, he thought. He would call Alison.

As he started to dial her number, the construct's face floated in his mind. Brian felt a rush of embarrassment as he remembered how exactly the construct had looked like Alison. He could not imagine her reaction if she discovered he had basically had VR sex with a version of her. He put the phone down. As he tried to figure out who to call, he checked his inbox until he found the paperwork from Red Door Saloon. He was able to print a list of items he would need. "Now if only they could tell me how I'm going to care for this baby," he muttered to himself.

Brian read through the pages, printing the items he thought he would need. As he got to the last page, he noticed a statement at the bottom.

THANK YOU FOR YOUR PURCHASE. WE HOPE YOU ENJOYED YOUR TIME AND LOOK FORWARD TO SEEING YOU AGAIN SOON AT THE RED DOOR SALOON.

"Chad!" Brian exclaimed as he jumped out of his seat. "This is all Chad's fault. He bought me the dumb experience. He got me into this. He can for sure get me out of it. I'm not doing this alone."

As the baby began to make noise, Brian realized he had spoken out loud. He sat back down, grabbing his phone.

"Chad, it's Brian," he stated, "I need you to come over as soon as you get this message. It is urgent. You need to come alone."

Brian hung up feeling calmer. He would demand that Chad help with all of this. It was all going to be fine.

Three hours later, Brian was walking the floor, jiggling the baby, when he heard the doorbell. Looking at his computer, he recognized Chad and buzzed him in. Brian had ordered all the items off the list and most had been delivered in the last three hours. His checking account had sizably dwindled and he was exhausted. The baby (he knew he needed to name her but that would just make this nightmare too real) had been fed and a clean diaper put on. But now she would not stop crying. The only solution was to walk and jiggle, walk and jiggle. The minute Brian stopped the baby would unleash a deafening cry that sounded as if it were coming from hundreds of babies.

When Chad walked in the door, Brian unleashed his frustrations. "This all your fault. I don't know what I'm doing. I never wanted a baby. But now I have one. I can't care for a baby. This is all too much. You created this mess. You have to help me. She won't stop crying. I can't stop walking. It is all just too much. I called you hours ago, where have you been?"

Chad stood with his mouth hanging open, his jade eyes wide in confusion and shock. He barely even registered what Brian was saying, he was so stupefied by seeing his friend carrying a baby. When Brian began to start his rant over, Chad started processing what Brian was saying. Brian did not get very far, before he broke in.

"Wait, I don't understand," he stated. "How is any of this my fault?"

Brian walked over and dumped the baby into Chad's arms not even waiting to ensure he would catch her. "She's from the VR sex club," Brian stated, as if that explained it all.

Chad furled his brow into a frown. "And?" he prompted.

"And it's your fault!" Brain exclaimed. "You have to help me. This is your fault."

Chad moved to the VR couch, the only place to sit besides at the computer desk. He shook his head. "I still don't understand. Start at the beginning."

Brian heaved a sigh. "I think she's finally sleeping. Don't wake her up."

Chad looked down at the baby in his arms. Her eyes were closed as she breathed deeply. Taking direction from Brian, he carefully placed her in a bassinet that only arrived a short time before he did. The baby stirred slightly, then kept sleeping. Chad let out the breath he didn't even know he had been holding. Turning, he stated, "Start at the beginning."

Brian sat in his chair and turned to face Chad. "You bought me a pass to that VR sex club."

Chad looked at Brian still confused. When Brian did not say any more, exasperated, Chad finally prompted, "I don't know what that has to do with this baby."

Brian raised his muddy brown eyes to meet Chad's bright green ones. "They asked a lot of questions. Some were quite personal." Brian lowered his eyes as his cheeks turned pink. "I got embarrassed and annoyed. I just started marking everything 'yes', without really reading it."

Chad's mouth dropped open. "You did what?"

"I just marked 'yes'."

"And how is that my fault?" Chad asked.

"I wouldn't have been there if not for you," Brian accused.

"So, let me get this straight. You have never had sex and are obsessed with women. You are so overly concerned with this that it ruins any chance you have to date. I try to help you out by buying you a pass. A pass that cost a lot of money I might add.

"You go to the club. That was your choice. Then when they ask you about sex. Sex that you want, you get too embarrassed and don't read all the questions," Chad paused to catch his breath. Continuing, his voice raised, "Then somehow this is all my fault? My fault? I can't believe I even tried to help you. My fault?"

As Chad's voice continued to get louder, the baby stirred again.

"Don't wake her up," Brian interrupted frantically. "I – I – Just don't."

Chad looked from the bassinet to Brian and back again. "I don't know what you are going to do, but I'm out. This is not my fault and the fact you would even consider it was-" Chad stopped. Taking a deep breath, he continued in a calmer voice, "-Brian, I would really like to help you, but somehow you are going to have to learn to help yourself first." Chad walked over to the bassinet. Looking down at the baby, he asked Brian, "What is her name?"

Brian sighed. "I don't know. I haven't given her one yet."

Chad shook his head and walked to the door. "Brian, you really need to figure this all out. It is time you grow up. If not for you, then at least for her."

Brian stared at the closed door after Chad left. He needed to grow up. He could not believe that Chad had said that. Chad who went out with a different girl every night. Chad who thought a major decision was which club to go to. Chad was telling him to grow up. But Chad was right about one thing. He was going to have to figure this out.

"I'm going to need a lot of grace to get through all of this," he thought remembering something Susan used to say.

Brian brightened as he thought about it. "Grace. I need Grace. That is what I will name her." With that, he turned around to the computer to fill out the forms now that he had her name, while Grace slept on in her crib.

Chapter Twenty-One

GRACE

Grace flipped through the holographic photo album, looking at the pictures from her childhood. Her dad had given it to her for her 15th birthday. She twirled her chestnut hair on her finger as she looked at the different scenes. The pictures started from when she was about 2 weeks old and ended two days before this birthday. She could remember her dad being so insistence at getting that last picture. At the time, she did not understand why he wanted one right then and there. When he had given her the album, it had all made sense.

Grace looked around her room. She was turning sixteen tomorrow, but her room was still much how it had been since early childhood. Her room was done in pink, purple, and white. Childhood colors to her mind. In the corner, she had a hanging net full of every stuffed animal she had ever been given. Her bed was made with frilly blankets, white with purple flowers and pink butterflies. Against one wall, her desk since she was eight held her brushes, makeup, school books, and other items. It was painted white with pink accents. Some days, Grace felt as if she was trapped in a cotton candy nightmare.

Grace frowned as she closed her hazel eyes. She had talked to her dad several times about changing her room, but he always said, "later." She knew what that actually meant, "never." Tomorrow she would turn 16. When would he start letting her make some of her own decisions? She was not a child anymore, but he never seemed to notice that. She took a deep breath and opened her eyes. Now was as good a time as any.

Grace walked out into the living room. She could barely remember the apartment they had lived in when she was little. Her dad had moved them to this house when she was five. The living room was not as sparse as the old apartment, but it still was pretty minimalist. When she had friends over, they often joked that no one lived in this room. She found her father sitting in front of his computer screen. She rolled her eyes and sighed. She couldn't really complain. He almost always had time for her and went to all her school activities. But sometimes, she thought, "he just needs to get a life. Maybe then he won't be so controlling with mine."

"Dad, I need to talk to you," she started.

Brian turned around in his chair. His brown eyes catching hers. "What?" he prompted.

"Now, don't get mad," she stated.

"Any conversation that starts with that sentence is unlikely to be a good one," Brian half joked as he arched an eyebrow at her. He brushed his hands through his short spiky hair. Grace had been unsure when he had come home with this new haircut, thinking he was trying to act and look too young. But it had grown on her and it did seem to really suit him.

"Dad," she complained, "I just mean hear me out. You tend to get upset and don't hear me. I really want to talk to you."

Brian just sat, waiting for her to continue. Grace huffed when she decided that he was not going to say anything.

"I turn sixteen tomorrow," she began waiting on her father's nod. "I will be moving to college in two years." Another nod from her father.

"Well, I just thought that maybe, you know, I could, like.... I don't know," Grace stammered getting frustrated with herself. She had practiced this like five thousand times. Now with her dad just staring at her, she could not even get the words out.

"I just thought it was time, that I was old enough, that I could start dating. You know." Grace finished in a rush.

Brian did not say a word and continued to just stare at her. Grace stared back a battle of wits between them. When Grace could not stand it any longer, she broke, "Say something," she demanded.

Brian took a deep breath and released it. "Am I allowed to talk now?"

Grace groaned. She knew where this was going.

"Yes."

"Then, the answer is no."

"But, Dad! This is ridiculous. You cannot keep me locked up in this house forever. I am going to be an adult soon. I should be allowed to date."

Brian simply replied, "No."

Grace huffed loudly, face flushing with anger. "Seriously. Is that all you can say? You just want to keep me a child forever. Well, I'm not a child. It is stupid I can't date. All my friends date. I bet you dated when you were my age."

"I didn't. I have never really dated."

"So you punish me and won't let me date? That is so unfair. I can't believe you are being this way," Grace raised her voice.

"There is no point in having this discussion until you can calm down. You are being childish, yet expecting me to treat you like you are an adult."

"Not an adult, but recognize that I am almost an adult."

Brian sighed, but kept a calm voice. Sometimes that is what infuriated Grace the most. No matter how upset he got or how heated their arguments, her father never showed much, if any, emotions.

Brian stated, "You are acting like a child. I'm not discussing this further with you. I told you my answer was 'no'. I cannot control what you do once you are an adult, but as long as you are a child living under my roof, the answer will always be 'no'."

Grace let out a scream of frustration as she threw the holographic album she did not even remember holding at him. "I hate you," she screamed as she stomped to her room and slammed her door. Brian got up and slowly walked over to the photo album and picked it up.

Chapter Twenty-Two

BRIAN

Brian sighed as he sat back down. Being a single father was hard. When Grace had been a baby, he had thought it would be impossible to ever learn everything he needed to know. She had seemed so small and fragile. Looking at the pictures, he smiled to remember how scared he was that he would break her.

But now, he almost wished he could return to those times. It had been so much easier. If only he had known. The directions from the VR company had been a good start. He had found a good daycare. The main provider, Miss Nancy, had helped and given him her number to call day or night. Brian had struggled, but when Grace had gazed at him with those big beautiful eyes full of love, his heart would melt. Looking at those pictures, he wondered how she had gone from that to this screaming ball of demands.

Brian continued to slowly flip through the pictures reliving highlights of their lives together. Soon after she turned two, he had gotten a work from home job. She still went to daycare two days a week, but most days she had been home with him. The picture of her sitting on the kitchen floor surrounded by every item she could pull out of the cupboards made him smile. That had been one of the last times he had called Miss Nancy.

Looking at her school pictures, he remembered how she had cried the first day of school. What Grace had never known was that once he was in his car, he had cried harder than her. Just when he thought he was really getting the parenting thing down, off to school she had went. His days had seemed so quiet and empty with her at school all day. But he had survived.

Brian turned to the picture of Grace's tenth birthday party. He could see a pony in the background. She had invited her whole classroom. They had pony rides for everyone. He knew that he had probably spoiled her and overdone it. But that had been such a fun day. However, Grace had overate on cake and ice cream. He had been up with her all night while she was sick. To this day, Grace had an aversion to peppermint ice cream.

Brian sighed as he kept reviewing the pictures. Each one a treasured moment of his life with Grace. She was so precious to him. The only things they ever really fought about were her mother and her dating. Grace had started pushing to know more about her mother while she had been doing a school project when she was in fifth grade. Two years ago, she had started asking to date. She had really started pushing in the last six months.

Brian rubbed his neck as he rolled it around, trying to release the tension in his back. He didn't want to be mean, but he knew how boys were. Grace didn't. He needed to protect her and keep her safe. What if she dated the wrong boy? What if she got her heart broken? What if an incel tried to date her? Too many things could go wrong. He did not want to upset her, but she could not be dating. He would have to talk to her later.

Brian waited until he had supper done to call upstairs to Grace. He hoped that eating a meal together would help them repair their relationship after the fight. He laid Grace's holographic book by her plate and dished up the food. It was times like these that single parenting was the hardest. Never having someone else to be the buffer between them and help them get over the hurt feelings and anger.

"Grace, are you coming down?" he called up the stairs.

"No."

"Grace, you have to eat."

"No."

"Grace, stop being stupid and come down here right now," Brain called getting frustrated.

"No."

He stood at the bottom of the stair and counted to ten. Then to twenty. It could never be simple. "Look, we have to talk. So either you can come down here, or I'm coming up there."

Brian waited, but only got silence. "Grace?" he called. Nothing.

Brian started up the stairs slowly. Halfway up, he remembered her book. He turned to get it when he heard her door open. Looking up, he could see her standing in the open door, back lit by her ceiling light. Her hair glowed almost a cinnamon color, the lighting bringing out the reds. He could see her "mother" in her maturing face. It took him by surprise making him catch his breath.

"I was just going back down to get your photo album. I had it by your plate," he explained.

Grace nodded and moved forward. "I will come down. I was just saying no because that's how you treat me."

Brian hid his face by looking down. He could see how rude it might seem to her, but he was her father. He had the right to say 'no'. "It's okay. I know you are mad, but I would like to talk to you-" he held up his hand as he could see Grace start to speak, "-and yes, I will say more than 'no'. "

Grace trailed her dad down the stairs. Brian grabbed her book off the table as they moved to the living room. Brian sat in his computer chair out of habit. Grace flopped gracelessly on the couch.

"I don't think I have ever seen you sit anywhere else," she commented.

Brian looked startled. "I never really think about it. I just sit here."

Grace stared at Brian with her intense eyes. He was always amazed at how they changed color with her mood. They were a vibrant brown with flecks of green and blue. The more you stared at them, the less you could say for sure what color they were. They suited her face. Brian knew he needed to start, but seemed at a loss for words.

"I really want to talk, but I'm not even sure where to start. Looking at your book it.."

Grace interrupted, "Sorry about that. I just was so mad. I didn't even remember I was holding it and then it was just flying out of my hands."

Brian continued, "It's okay. It was nice to look through it, even if it was not nice the way I received it. It gave me a chance to look back. It has not always been easy being a single dad. But I have always loved you.

"Sometimes it gets so hard to make decisions about what is best for you. I just want to keep you safe. To have you be happy. I know I can be hard sometimes, but I just know all the bad in the world."

Grace answered, "I know you are just trying to protect me. But, Dad, I can't live in a bubble forever. Someday I have to meet guys. I have to date. I love you and all, but I really don't want to live with you for the rest of my life."

Brian chuckled at her comment. "Would that really be so bad? You could take care of me when I'm feeble with old age."

Grace threw a couch cushion at him. "Dad, be serious. I'm not living with you. Besides, you will never be too old."

Brian smiled as he caught the cushion. "So do you have a guy in mind?"

"No, not really." Grace got a sweet smile. "I do have a friend named, Alex. But I don't know. I'm not sure about him."

"So this dating is more like an idea. Can you go on a date sometime? Not something you have a plan to do right now?" Brian questioned.

Grace tilted her head in thought, her eyes looking upwards. "I don't really have anyone I want to date right now. I would just like to know that I could go on a date if someone wants to go out with me."

Brian felt relief as his whole body relaxed. He did not have to worry about her dating immediately. "Grace, you are a beautiful, smart, funny, great young lady. It is not a question of if someone will want to go out with you, it is a question of if you would want to go out with them. When you are ready to date, you will be able to have the pick of any guy."

Grace smiled. "Does that mean I can date?"

Brian felt trapped. He had walked into this. Trying to get back to safer ground, he answered, "I am not saying 'yes'." To Grace's instant frown, he quickly added, "But I'm not saying 'no'."

"So what does that mean?"

"It means that when you have a specific boy you want to date, come talk to me. I am not saying I will say 'yes', but I will consider it."

Chapter Twenty-Three

GRACE

Grace sat there listening to her father ramble on. She was only barely listening. Her mind was still focused on the "you can date if" part of what he had said. She thought about her friend Alex. Did she want to date him? What about James? Who did she really want to date?

"Dad," she interrupted, "how do you know who you want to date?"

Brian stopped in mid-sentence. "Umm, well, that's a good question. Do you have someone in mind?"

Grace thought about her friend. "I don't know. Maybe. I have a friend that is nice. We hang together and stuff. But I'm not sure. Sometimes he's kind of out there."

Brian stared at his daughter. "Well, it is your choice. You are in control." Brian launched into more incel rhetoric, capturing Grace's attention this time. She listened as he talked about how she could have any guy she chose.

"But what if he's already dating someone else?" she interrupted again.

Brian furrowed his brow in concentration. "I guess I have never really thought about that. But you know I'm not sure it matters.

There are so many guys that don't have girlfriends, you definitely can have the pick of them."

Grace sat there tuning her dad out as she turned those words over and over in her mind. Tomorrow she would go to school and find someone. She couldn't wait.

Grace took one more look in the mirror as she applied pink lip gloss to her rosebud lips. Her chestnut hair was slicked back into a high ponytail. She had already made her thick lashes longer with mascara. Her hazel eyes were looking more green today with her careful application of makeup. She widened them and practiced making shy smiles. The whole time her dad's words kept running through her head, "you can have any guy you want."

Grace smiled one last time at herself in the mirror. She grabbed her book bag and headed out. Today was the day. It was time to find someone to date.

Grace got to school and went to her locker. Her best friend, Sandy, had a locker right beside her. She smiled at her. Sandy looked Grace up and down.

"You seem extra special today," Sandy commented.

Grace smiled. "Dad gave in. Well, sort of. But he said if I had someone I wanted to date, he was willing to meet him and consider it."

Sandy laughed. "So what? You are going to get a guy today."

Grace smiled. "Yup. I think it is time, don't you?"

Sandy smiled again. Sandy was tall and built similar to a guy, straight up and down with no curves. She was not ugly, but her face was not memorable in anyway, either. She was a great friend – kind, generous, and caring, but nothing that would draw the attention of a teenage boy. In fact, Sandy would often fade into the background or just follow in Grace's shadow.

"If only it was that simple," Sandy commented, thinking of all the boys she would like to date, while knowing she never would.

Grace looked at her. She had never really considered why Sandy never had a boyfriend. She looked around at the hall teeming with other students hurrying to class. She did wonder now.

"I don't know. I guess I will find out," Grace answered her.

Sandy glanced behind Grace. "Don't look now, but here comes that loser."

Grace looked over her shoulder. "Who?"

"Alex," Sandy answered. "I don't know why you hang out with him. He's such a loser. All those things he says about women. Seriously, Grace. He is so weird."

Alex walked over. "Hey, you are looking nice today," he stated.

Grace looked at Alex trying to see him through Sandy's eyes. He walked with his permanent slouch and wore the same typical clothes. His blue jeans were ripped and his T-shirt had holes. His light brown hair looked like it had not been washed in a few days and hung limply around his face appearing a shade or two darker. She really didn't even know why she was friends with him. He was nice, but he could be kind of weird at times. But he was smart and fun to talk with.

"Hey, Alex, did you get your chemistry homework done?" Grace asked.

Alex nodded and glanced sideways at Sandy. The two of them did not always get along. When Alex made weird statements about women, Grace usually just ignored them, but Sandy would get into arguments with him.

"Hello, Sandy," he stated.

Sandy reached into her locker, trying to avoid him. Grace gave her a slight nudge. "Oh, hello, Alex," she finally answered.

Grace smiled. "I'm glad you got the homework done. I thought it was going to be easy, but boy it wasn't."

Alex nodded again. "Do you want to hang during lunch?"

Grace shook her head. "I can't today. But I will catch up with you later. I have got to go. I'm going to be late to class."

Grace hurried off down the hallway and did not hear Sandy and Alex keep talking.

"What has gotten into her?" Alex asked.

"She is on a mission," Sandy answered.

"A mission?"

Sandy just shook her head and headed to class. "Nothing."

Grace got to her first class of the day. It was early, but other students were already in the room milling around. She saw James sitting at his desk reviewing his work. To Grace, James was the most gorgeous boy she had ever seen. She had never really talked to him, but with her dad's words from last night in her head, she decided she would do it now.

Grace plopped down in the desk besides James. He barely even noticed. She sat there awkwardly, not knowing what to say. The longer she sat, the more awkward she felt. James did not seem to even notice her. Finally, Grace could not handle it anymore. She blurted out, "Hey there, James. I thought I would see if you wanted to study together sometime."

James looked straight at Grace as if seeing her for the first time. He looked perplexed. "Study? Why would we do that?"

Grace swallowed hard. She didn't know what to say. "I don't know. I just get together with friends sometimes and…." she trailed off.

James blinked his eye and continued to examine her. "Why would you want to study with me? Why not study with these other friends?"

Grace flushed red. Her mind raced as she tried to figure out what to say. "I just thought.. Well you know… I just… Well.. We could you know…"

James continue to show no emotion on his face as he stared at Grace. His face remained placid and his voice even. "No, I really don't know. You don't seem to be capable of telling me."

Grace's skin reddened even darker. She scrambled to come up with something, anything. This was not going how she expected. It was supposed to be easier than this. Her dad had said it would be.

"I just thought it would be fun to spend time together. And you know, get to know each other," she finally blurted out.

James slowly cocked his head to one side and let his eyes roam up and down Grace's body. When they came back to rest on her face, he took in her embarrassment. With a small smile, he stated, "And why would I want to do that? "

Grace was instantly mortified. She didn't know what had went wrong, but she could feel tears springing up in her eyes. This was not how things were supposed to go. What had she done wrong?

Grace jumped up. Fighting back tears, she ran from the room. Bumping into Sandy in the doorway, Grace told her, "I feel sick. I'm going to the nurse's office and then going home."

Sandy tried to stop her. But Grace shoved past her and fled down the hallway.

Chapter Twenty-Four

GRACE

Grace got home from school, fled to her room, and threw herself down on her bed. Her eyes were red from crying and her throat felt scratchy. She didn't know what had happened, but obviously she had failed. She did even want to return to school. She was sure everyone knew what had happened. She would be the laughing stock of the school.

After a while, Grace calmed down. She prowled around the house trying to find something to do to take her mind off everything. She went into her dad's room and got out some old photo albums. Taking them downstairs, she curled up on the couch and started looking through them. Many of them were of her father and Chad when they were in college. She knew he had known Chad forever, but had not realized they had known each other even in college.

Looking through the photos, she came across some from her father's first job. She recognized some of the people. There Jerry, that her dad still had contact with today. Chad, of course, was in several of the pictures. But, one picture took Grace's breath away. She found a picture of two women sitting together laughing. The one woman wore dark glasses that hid her face. But it was the other woman that made her gasp.

Grabbing the photo, she ran to her bedroom mirror and held it up to her face. The resemblance was obvious. It could easily be a photo of her in a few years. Grace looked at the back of the picture, but nothing was written on the back. She raced back downstairs and snatched up the photo album. Her hands shaking as she looked for more pictures or captions that would tell her who this woman was.

After pouring through all the albums, Grace had found two more pictures, but still had no clue who the mystery woman was. The only photos were from before her birth. Was this her mother? Who was she? Had she died? All thoughts of school, James, and her fiasco with him went out of her mind as she tried to figure out the answers to those questions.

Grace looked at her father's computer set up. The school knew her dad worked from home, which is why they had let her come home sick today. What they didn't know was that today was one of the few days he had to go into the office. She knew he had a way to scan photos into his computer and then search for other images throughout the web and social media. But she was not supposed to touch his computer.

Her father had gotten her a computer of her own after finding her trying to use his one night. He had explained that his was never to be touched. It had "Very Important Stuff" on it. Grace knew her computer was not as equipped as his. She doubted she would be able to run a facial match search on hers. But did she dare use his?

Grace sat there staring at her dad's computer for a long time. She really wasn't sure when she made the actual decision to use it, but she suddenly found herself sitting in his chair turning the system on. She decided she would use his scanner and email the photo to herself. Then she would attempt a search on her computer.

Looking at the clock, she knew that she was getting limited on time. If her computer wasn't able to do it, she would not have time to come back without fearing she would get caught. But she knew that her dad would be less suspicious of her using the scanner. She had been given permission in the past for homework. She would just have to convince him that is what she did this time.

Grace was sitting on the couch with her feet tucked up under her when her father returned home. She had the photo albums sitting beside her and some sheets printed out from her computer. The house was bathed in twilight as Grace had never turned on the lights while she was sitting there.

Brian walked in and snapped on the lights. "Grace, you startled me. I didn't see you sitting there." He turned towards his computer and started dealing with the items in his briefcase.

Grace asked, "Why did you lie to me?"

Brian stopped what he was doing and turned to her. "Lie to you. I don't understand. I didn't lie to you."

Grace stated, "You told me that I could have any guy I wanted. You said, my being able to date was just based on if the guy was single. Well, James is single, but he sure isn't going to date me."

"Grace, honey, I am not understanding what you are talking about," her dad answered.

Grace stood up and walked towards him. "You said that I could have any boy I wanted. Well, I wanted James, but when I tried to talk to him, it was awful." Tear slowly rolled down Grace's cheeks as she remembered the whole encounter.

"I dressed up special. I did my hair and makeup. I did everything right and he just treated me like a pest. He was mean." Grace was sobbing by the time she got the last words out.

Brian moved towards her, but Grace put her hand out in front of her. "No, Daddy, I want to know why you lied to me? Why? Did you want this to happen so that I would never date? Why?"

Brian sat back down in his chair, horrified. "I didn't lie. In my experience, most girls, especially really pretty girls like you, can date whoever they want. I honestly thought you would have no problems meeting a guy and going out with him."

Grace shook her head as her father was speaking. She knew he hadn't really wanted her to get hurt, but she wasn't ready to let it go.

"But that's not how it works. My friend, Sandy, has never had a boyfriend. Not even someone she just hangs with like I hang with Alex. She is really nice, but she's not very pretty. None of the boys like her. They call her names. You never go on dates, either. I don't think you really even know anything about dating."

Chapter Twenty-Five

BRIAN

Brian looked at Grace aghast. His mind in a whirl. Was it true? Did he really not know how dating worked? Were there women out there who were just as lonely as he was? Brian looked at Grace and thought about some of his co-workers. Cindy was single. Jan was twice divorced. He did not think either of them ever dated. He knew he had never considered dating either of them.

Brian lowered his eyes, rubbing them. Maybe he was just as bad as the women he accused. He was picky and only willing to date the "good ones". Brian shook his head and looked at Grace still sobbing in front of him. He would have to think about all of this later. Right now, he needed to help Grace.

Brian stood back up and moved towards Grace. Gathering her up in his arms, he moved her to the couch and sat holding her. "You know, honey, you might be right. I don't really date, never really have. I am probably not the best to ask for dating advice. I'm so sorry. I really did think what I was saying was true."

Grace sobbed. "Well, it's not."

"I can see that now. I am so sorry this happened." Brian sat there stroking her hair and trying to calm her down. "I don't know why that boy didn't want to date you. You are smart, and cute, and funny. He has to be really stupid to not want to date you."

Grace giggled slightly, her tears slowing down. "Dad, he's one of the smartest boys in my class."

Brian hugged her. "Well, he can't be too smart. He doesn't want to date you. I think that says most of the boys in your class are not too smart."

Grace sighed, "Dad, don't say that."

"Well, you know your dad will always think you are the greatest."

Grace gave him a small smile.

"Can I get you anything?" Brian asked.

Grace nodded and asked for some lemonade. Brian got up and got a drink. Coming back, he noticed all the photo albums. "What have you been up to?"

Grace quickly moved them out of his reach. "I came home from school. I told the nurse I was sick. I was just too upset to be at school."

Brian nodded. "I understand."

Grace shuffled through the papers. Finding the one she wanted. "So I was looking through old photo albums and found some of when you were in college. Who is Alison Williams?" Grace asked holding up the photo with Alison's information. "Is she my mother?"

Brian froze. Confronted with the photo held by Grace, he could see what Grace had seen hours earlier. The resemblance was uncanny. It was as if Grace had gotten all her DNA from the Alison construct and none from him. His mind went blank. He didn't know what to say. Alison was not really her mother, but that explanation was not one he wanted to have with his teenage daughter. How to explain that she had been conceived in VR through tech? He still didn't quite understand the whole process.

But he couldn't completely deny it either. Alison had been the inspiration for his experience, and it was a version of her DNA that had been created and used. As the thoughts kept running through his mind, he didn't notice that Grace was getting more and more upset with him. Tuning back in, he found her yelling at him.

"I have a right to know who my mother is. You have kept this from me long enough. You have kept her from me long enough. I will see her no matter what you say. You cannot stop me."

Brian was terrified. How had Grace figured this out? He had to stop this now. He could not let her contact Alison.

Brian thought back over the last sixteen years. He had stayed friends with Chad, but limited his interactions with Alison. He rarely sent them photos of Grace and as she aged, he had sent even fewer. He had limited face to face interactions when he could. He sometimes thought Chad or Alison might be suspicious because he had caught both staring at Grace thoughtfully at times. But he had never discussed her mother with them.

One night right before Chad and Alison got married, Brian and Chad had gone out in the "real world" and got sloppy drunk. Chad had confessed his love for Alison and how she was his princess. He apologized over and over to Brian for "stealing her from him," until Brian had finally told him that "you can't steal what the other person never had."

Chad had thought that was funny and giggled about it the rest of night. At one point, he confronted Brian and said, "But you must have had her once, or where else did Grace come from?"

Brian had stammered that he did not know what Chad was talking about. That was as close as they had ever come to discussing Grace's mother. Brian had been relieved when Chad did not seem to remember or pretended not to recollect the conversation the next day. Chad and Alison had a son who was about a year younger than Grace. Through the years, Alison had drifted out of Brian's life as she became more involved in raising her son and her career.

Brian and Chad continued to hang out, but usually to watch football or drink beer, or both. Grace was often not around. Brian encouraged that. He could see how much like Alison she looked as she grew older. He had lived in fear that Chad or Alison would see this and confront him. He had never dreamed it would be Grace herself that would notice.

Brian had been ignoring Grace as the past ran through his mind. She had continued to demand answers and was getting angrier the more he did not answer. Her final statement caught his attention. "Maybe I should just call her if you are not going to talk to me."

Brian opened his mouth to stop her, when the doorbell rang. Brian and Grace both looked at each other and then at the door. Both were confused. Almost no one ever came over. People would screen. You would meet up in the real world or VR. But almost never did people come over. And never without screening first.

Brian panicked. Somehow Alison knew what was going on and was here to confront him. "Don't answer that!" he yelled.

Grace looked at him like he was crazy. Pointing to the screen. "It's my friend, Alex," she said.

Brian drew in a deep breath. Saved literally by the bell. He could avoid talking to Grace about her mother and get to know this young man. "Sorry. I don't know why I said that. Go ahead and let him in."

Grace nodded, but hardened her eyes until they were like stone. "But this discussion is not over. And you be nice to him."

Brian slowly walked back to his computer desk and finished putting his work papers away. He moved as if he had aged 15 years since their conversation had started. He could not believe that Grace knew her mother. He would be forced to have a very painful discussion with her, but he just did not know how. He was going to need to warn Chad and Alison. Sitting down in his chair, he rubbed his temples feeling one of his headaches starting again.

"Dad," he heard Grace say. Looking up, he saw her followed by a young man. He slouched as he walked and seemed sullen. "This is Alex. He brought me my homework since I came home sick today."

Grace turned to Alex. "Would you like to stay and study together?"

Alex dipped his head. "I don't know. I wasn't really planning on staying."

Grace reached out for her books, patting Alex on the arm while she did. Brian watched every movement like a hawk. He noticed how Alex seemed to straighten and looked less sullen when Grace touched him.

"You are welcome to stay," Grace commented glancing her at her father. "I'm sure I might have questions you can help me with."

Brian looked from Alex to Grace. "Thank you, young man," he said. Gesturing towards the dining room table. "Would you like to have some lemonade or brownies while you go over everything with Grace?"

Alex brightened immediately. He smiled at Grace, keeping ahold of the books, he walked towards the table. "I would love some lemonade if it is not too much trouble. Grace is much smarter than me," he stated, "but I can try and help."

Grace smiled as Alex pulled out a chair for her. "I'm sure you can explain to me what I missed."

Brian relaxed. He went to the kitchen bringing back a drink for Alex and a plate of brownies. Sitting them down, he announced, "I have some work to do, but let me know if you need me." Excusing himself, Brian moved back to his computer.

He sat there doing busy work as he watched Grace and Alex interacting. It was obvious that Alex liked Grace. It was just as obvious that Grace had no clue. She was nice and polite, but showed no interest in him. Brian wondered if she truly was not interested, or just focused on her schoolwork.

Brian invited Alex to stay for supper, but he declined saying he had to get home. Once Alex left, Grace continued to work on her homework as Brian cooked. As he sat the food on the table, she looked up. "Thank you for letting Alex stay. That was really nice."

Brian smiled at her. "He seems like a nice boy. And it seems like he really likes you."

Grace frowned. "Likes me? What are you talking about? We are just friends."

"It is obvious. He smiles more when you talk to him. He can't stop looking at you. And, most important of all, he sat here doing homework with you. That young man likes you."

Grace continued to look perplexed. "He has never said anything."

Brian sat down by her and began dishing up his food. "He just seemed like a good person to date."

"But, Dad, he's weird. Everyone thinks he is a loser. Why would I want to date him?"

Brian answered, "What is weird about him? Why is he a loser?"

Thoughtfully, Grace considered her father's questions. "I don't really know. He does have some strange ideas. He likes to talk about how girls are mean and about how they pick who they date. He talks about how things should be 'like they used to be'. "

"What does he mean by that?"

Grace answered, "I'm not sure. I think he means like where people married one person for life and didn't get divorced or bounce around from person to person. I never really asked him."

Brian nodded. He kind of liked this Alex. He could hear himself saying these things. The idea of being faithful was a good one, but he could see how that would not be popular among students Alex's age. No wonder he was being called weird and a loser.

"Do you like him?" Brian asked.

Grace shrugged her shoulders and pursed her lips, "I have never really thought about it. He's smart and funny, when he's not being weird. He's always nice and polite to me. I have fun when we hang out. But I don't know. He's not cute like James."

"But is how he looks that important?"

Grace looked embarrassed. "I know the correct answer is 'no', but I can't help it. I really thought James was cute. Alex could be cute, maybe, if he put in effort. I don't know."

Brian looked at this daughter. "Well, you could go out with him and see how it goes. It might surprise you."

Grace looked startled. "A date? You mean you would let me go out with him? For real?"

Brian smiled. "Yes, I think it would be an excellent idea."

Grace jumped up and started scrambling up the stairs. "I'm going to go call him right now. I wonder what we could do." Stopping at the top of the stairs, turning back to Brian. "We are still going to discuss my mother. Don't think you can buy me off with allowing me to date."

Brian gulped. "That's not what I was doing. But-" he held up his hand as Grace tried to interrupt, "-this does not involve just you. I need to make some calls before we discuss things further."

Grace hardened her face, squinting her eyes at her father. "I'm not sure I believe you. But I will wait.

For now."

Brian gave a sigh of relief as Grace turned and headed to her room. Things were going to get very awkward very soon.

Chapter Twenty-Six

BRIAN

Brian finished tidying up the kitchen and dishes. Walking slowly to the computer, he knew he could not put this call off any longer. He sat down and shook his head. His hands trembled as he slowly put in the number and waited for the phone to ring. He tried to think when was the last time he had called. It had been a few months at least.

Brian drummed his fingers on the desk, his stomach churning as he waited for the phone to answer. Then, suddenly, Chad was there, looking as good as ever.

"Hey, Brian, what's up? Long time no hear from," Chad answered.

"Is Alison around?" Brian asked.

Chad looked at Brian. "Why are you asking? You never ask about her?"

Brian took a deep breath. "I need to talk to you about something and I don't want her to overhear."

Chad continued to look uncertain. "Brian, what is going on?"

Brian decided to just jump in. "It's Grace. She knows. Well, she doesn't completely know. But she thinks she knows. It's a mess. She is going to call Alison if we don't do something."

Chad took a moment processing everything that Brian just said. "Alison is out with friends. Mike is in his room doing homework. No one is going to hear. But what do you mean she knows? She knows what? You are going to have to make more sense."

Brian sat still afraid to move. What was he going to say? He didn't really even understand it exactly, now he had to explain to Chad, about his wife.

"Well, remember, this was a long time ago," Brian started.

Chad nodded. "Yes, get on with it."

Chad would never make this easy. "You and Alison had just started dating. You had sent me that VR sex club ticket. I did use it. That's where Grace came from." Brian kept his eyes on his keyboard, glancing at Chad as he spoke. Chad's face went white at being reminded where Grace came from.

Chad spoke as the silence drew out, "I still don't understand what that has to do with Alison. I already knew that is where Grace came from. I have never told anyone. Not so much for you, as for Grace."

Brian nodded. "I thank you for that. But I never did explain the process to you."

Chad interrupted in a clipped voice, "I know how babies are made, Brian. I understand sex. I'm still not sure why we are having this conversation."

Brian put his face in his hands and rubbed his face. "Chad, please. This is horrible enough, just let me talk. Please."

Chad gave a sharp nod.

Brian continued, "I won't begin to say I understand that tech. But, somehow, they created a synthetic egg based on DNA that was coded to look like the avatar that I created. That was mixed with my DNA to create Grace," Brian paused to make sure Chad was understanding.

Chad motioned for Brian to continue.

"Some children end up looking up more like one parent than the other. That's what happened with Grace. She looks more like 'her mother'," Brian stated, using air quotes. Brian took another quick look at Chad. His face was frozen in a grimacing mask, even whiter than before. He seemed to know where this was going.

Brian pushed on, knowing he had to get it all out. "Grace was home today from school sick. Well, she wasn't really sick. A boy at school was mean to her and she came home crying. Anyway, she was going through old photo albums from when we were in college.

"She found a picture of Susan and Alison. She realized she looks almost exactly like Alison when she saw it. She is now determined to find her mother and meet her."

Chad blanched to the point his skin seemed almost translucent. His voice came out in a very quiet deathly whisper through clenched teeth, "You based your avatar on my wife. You had sex with my wife?" Chad continued as his voice raised. "Grace looks like Alison because half her DNA is based on her being Alison's daughter. You had sex with my wife and hid this from us for years!" By the last word, Chad was yelling.

Brian hunched down in his chair. "She wasn't your wife at the time. If you remember, I had been trying to date her and you took her from me."

Chad put his hands up to ward off Brian's words and clenched his fists. His face turning red. "This is not my fault. You will not blame this on me. You had sex with my wife. With a fake version of my wife, in VR. What was it? A chance to get back at me? At her?"

Brian put his elbows on the table and put his head in his hands. Rubbing his face, he mumbled, "I didn't mean it. I really didn't mean it. I never met to hurt anyone."

Chad interrupted his rambling, "Then you better explain."

Brian looked up at him. "The VR asked for my perfect partner. It had me chose a basic construct and then design it. I was giving instructions and only halfway paying attention. Suddenly, Alison's face was staring back at me from the screen. I realized that I had described her without meaning to.

"I thought about changing the construct, but then I didn't. You and her had just started dating. I was heartbroken, or at least I thought I was. I was like, who will ever know. It wasn't like I was really having sex with her. It was more like I was just borrowing her face. She would never know. "

"That makes it all better," Chad interjected.

"I know, I know. But, at the time, I was angry and hurt. I didn't think anyone would ever know."

Chad cut in again, "Brian, that's not an excuse."

Brian sighed, "I know that it's not an excuse. I am not that person anymore. I'm just trying to explain and let you know what I was thinking. I wasn't wanting to get back at anyone. I just wanted to be happy. If only for a short time and only in VR."

Chad sat for a long time and finally nodded. "So, then you clicked the pregnancy option. So, then there was Grace. I always thought she looked familiar. But I just never thought about Alison. I mean I knew Alison was not her mother."

Brian nodded. "But now she thinks Alison is her mother and I have to figure out how to tell her. I have to figure out how to tell Alison. I wanted to let you know first. You at least know where she came from. But Grace and Alison have no clue. How do I explain to my daughter she was a mistake because I was too embarrassed to pay attention to what I was doing?"

At that point, Chad's eyes widened and he looked as terrified as Brian felt. Chad pointed behind Brian.

Brian swiveled around in his chair to find that Grace had crept down the stairs. He did not know how much she had heard, but obviously she had heard the last part. She was crying. "I'm just a computer mistake. You never wanted me."

Brain tried to talk to her, "Grace, that's not true. Let me explain."

Grace yelled, "I don't want to hear anything you have to say. Leave me alone. I have no mother and now you are not my father. You lied to me my whole life."

With those words, she ran to the front door and left. Chad cleared his throat. Brian turned back to the screen.

"You seem to have enough on your plate. You need to go talk to her. I don't like what you did. But I will talk to Alison. I think she has suspected. But, like me, she just didn't know how. You are going to have to face up to her at some point. But you need to deal with your daughter now."

Brian nodded and logged off.

Chapter Twenty-Seven

GRACE

Grace ran down the street, not paying attention to where she was going. Her father's words pounding through her head in time with her feet on the concrete. Her ponytail bouncing on her back.

"Synthetic egg. Mistake. No mother."

Grace was not sure what these words meant. But somehow her father had made a mistake and gotten stuck with her. The man that she loved and trusted had never wanted her. As her anger grew, she pushed on farther and faster into the night, her breath coming in gasps. Finally, Grace's footsteps slowed as she became exhausted.

Looking around, Grace did not recognize any of the stores. She was not sure where she was. Walking slowly trying to catch her breath, she walked to the street corner hoping she would know the street names. She had left the house so fast, she had left her phone at home. Right now, she just wanted to figure out where she was and where she would go from here.

At the street corner, she discovered that she was only a few blocks from Alex's home. As she walked in that direction, her pace kept slowing. She was unsure if she really wanted to go to his house. What would she even say to him? "Hey, Alex, I just found out my dad never wanted me. I was a VR mistake made to look like some girl that wouldn't date him."

Even just thinking those words brought fresh tear streaming down her face. When she had found that picture, she had been so full of hope. Her dad was great, or at least he had been until all of this. But a mom. A real life, honest to goodness mom. She had been so excited to meet this Alison person and find out all about her. She never dreamed that she never really had a mom and that is why her father had kept this all from her.

At the next street corner, Grace came to a stop. Alex had been so cool coming to her house with her homework. She had been coming downstairs to tell her dad about their plans and get his approval for their date when she found him on the phone with Chad. She had not even gone back to her room. Alex was probably wondering what happened. She just couldn't turn up at his house like this.

Grace briefly considered walking to Sandy's house, but she was not real sure exactly how to get there. Besides, what would she say to her. Granted it was not as bad as telling the boy you wanted to date, but still. How do you even begin to be "normal" friends after that?

Grace slowly turned around and began to walk back home. It was getting dark and the wind was blowing her hair all around her face where it came loose from her ponytail. She dreaded talking to her father, but she knew she could not hide forever. Still, she didn't want to get home any faster than she had to.

As she walked, Grace's feelings bounced between tears and sadness, to angry and ranting under her breath, to fears of what she would learn from her dad when she got home. Grace rehearsed in her mind things she wanted to say to her father. But without knowing what he would say back, she really did not feel prepared.

When Grace finally turned down her walkway towards her front door, she felt exhausted. The run and all the emotions coursing through her had drained all her energy. She felt as if she could sleep for a month. But she knew she had to get this over with.

Slowly she climbed her front steps, opened the front door and silently slipped inside. The house was dark and quiet. She stood in the entrance way peering around. She did not see her dad anywhere. She started to tip toe towards the stairs, thinking she could sneak to her room and avoid her father for tonight. As she turned to head up them, he came out of the kitchen, not seeing her.

Grace took the moment to watch him. Her dad was walking as if he had aged twenty years since this afternoon. He walked hunched over with his head bent. His movements were slow and stiff as if his joints were almost rusted in place. Grace could see new lines on his face and his eyes appeared puffy as if he had been crying, also. Grace had never stopped to think about him and his point of view. All the years carrying that secret.

She felt her anger stir as she thought about the secret and how it had been kept from her. But looking at her father's obvious dejection, she wondered what the cost to him had been. She turned towards the living room.

Brian heard rustling and looked towards the stairs. "Grace, you are back," he stated, his voice quiet and hoarse.

"Yes. I didn't have anywhere else to go," she commented. "Who can I tell that I'm an unwanted VR mistake?"

Brian flinched as if she had hit him across the face. He stepped back towards his chair almost falling as it slid. "That is not really true. I'm not sure what you heard Chad and I saying, but I think we need to talk. I should have had this talk with you a long time ago, but it is embarrassing and not really something a father wants to talk to a daughter about."

Grace moved silently to the couch and sat down. Slipping her shoes off, she tucked her feet under her and pulled a blanket across her lap. She never took her eyes off her father, but she also did not say a word. She sat there calmly waiting for him to continue.

Brian had trouble knowing where to start. He opened his mouth as if to speak and closed it several times. Finally, he was able to get started. "This was a long time ago. I was a different person then. I was a different person because you made me a better person. It is kind of in the middle, but I want to start with your name."

"Grace," Grace said. "I have always wondered why you named me that."

Brian continued, "I was a hot mess back then. I didn't believe in myself. Always doubting myself. I got passed over for a promotion at work and went back and forth between that anger I didn't get it and believing I should never get one because I wasn't good enough.

"My dating life was a nonexistent. I tagged along with Chad to VR clubs and always got left by him when he would drop to the real world to hook up. I really had nothing going for me in part because I just didn't think I deserved it.

"Then you came along."

Grace interrupted, "I didn't just come along. I had sex ed at school. I know where babies come from. Or at least I thought I did."

Brian sighed. "It was a tech thing, that I didn't even know was possible. I don't know if it is still in use or not. To be honest, I have not really done much VR since I have been parenting you. Can I please tell this the way I want?" Brian asked.

Grace stared at him with no emotion on her face, eyes blank. Finally, she nodded. "As long as I get to ask questions when you are done if I don't feel as if you answered everything."

Brian gave a quick sharp nod. "Let's see. Yes, I was a hot mess. It was a horrible time for me. No surprise, I really didn't date much.

"Anyway, when I found out about you, I will admit that I freaked out. In fact, I freaked out a lot. I didn't even know that VR sex could lead to a baby. I still won't claim to completely understand the mechanics of it all. If you want to know more, I have some websites I researched."

Grace tilted her head forward showing acceptance. She really did not want to have to discuss sex with her father, let alone his own sex life. Just the thought of him having sex, even in VR, made her want to vomit.

"Ew, Dad, I don't need all those details," Grace commented.

Brian continued, "I had no choice with you. I had to improve and change and grow as a person. I had this little being that was completely dependent on me. I made the comment when I realized that you were mine and I had to accept that I really needed some grace to get me through all of this. That's when it hit me. You are my grace. You were what would drive me to be a better person.

"So, yes, you were not planned. But the truth is many children are born all the time that are not planned. That does not mean they are unloved. And yes, your conception and birth are not quite the norm, but that again does not mean you are not loved."

Brian lifted his eyes to meet Grace's and she could see the tears welling up and sliding down his cheeks as he continued, "I have loved you from the first moment I met you. I may have been petrified to be your father, but I still loved you. I wish I would have told you all of this sooner, but I'm still that scared young man some days. It is no excuse, but… Sometimes, I just can't help it."

Grace watched her father's emotions playing across his face. A part of her was still deeply hurt, but she could see that her father had never intended harm. She could see that he was hurting along with her.

"It's okay, Daddy," she said in a quiet little voice. "I won't say that I completely understand. I'm sure that I will have questions later. But I know you love me." With those words, Grace got up and walked across the floor to her father's chair. Bending down, she gave him a small kiss on the cheek. Brian reached up and grabbed her in a tight hug and pulled her down on his lap. He held and hugged her like when she was a small baby.

Grace snuggled down into his lap and felt safe like when she was little. She could not imagine life without her father. He had always been there for her. She could feel anger still tugging at her, but she really didn't care at this moment.

Chapter Twenty-Eight

BRIAN

Brian had sat there with Grace for a long time. After she went to bed, he sat staring at nothing. He knew he really needed to talk to Alison, but he knew it was going to be horrible. What he had done was unforgivable. Waiting would not make it any better, as things with Grace had shown him. But he really didn't feel he could handle any more after this day. The boy at school, meeting Alex, telling Chad, and finally Grace finding out. It was just too much.

Brian jumped as he heard the alert for an incoming call. Looking at his screen, he saw that Alison was calling. He hung his head. He knew where this was going. Pushing accept, he steeled himself.

Alison appeared on screen, she looked as beautiful as ever. He gazed at her as she frowned intently at him.

"Chad told me everything," she opened with. "I don't even know where to begin. The fact that you would do this. And keep it a secret. It is like you took something from me. I can't even begin to describe how I feel. Shit, I don't even know how I feel. But you betrayed me. You betrayed our friendship. With each day you kept the secret, you betrayed me a little more."

Alison paused for a breath. Her words cut through Brian, but more than anything, the cold iron in her voice told him he had hurt her deeply. Deeply enough that she was keeping all emotion out of her voice. He sat there waiting. He knew she wasn't done and at this moment nothing he said would matter.

Alison continued speaking, "It is like you stole into my room and had sex with me while I was sleeping. I keep picturing it in my mind and wondering if you have secretly thought about it when we were together. Did you ever wonder how it was compared to me? Did you think it was the same as having sex with me? I ....," she came to a sputtering halt. Brian could see tears welling up in her eyes.

"Don't cry, don't cry, don't cry," he thought. He knew how much she hated to cry and how much worse it would make this situation. If she cried in front of him now, when she was so hurt and angry with him, Brian knew it would take that much longer before she ever forgave him. If she ever did.

Alison resumed her ranting once she had her tears under control. Brian sat and listened respectfully. She deserved that. When she finally finished, she demanded, "What do you have to say for yourself?"

"Nothing," Brian answered.

"Nothing!" she screeched finally losing control. "Nothing?"

Brian tried again, "I have nothing to say, because there is nothing to say. I'm deeply sorry, but that does not change what I did. What I did was wrong and everything else you said. I have no excuses and no way to go back and change it. I cannot fix it or change how you feel. I violated your trust and your privacy. You are right it was a deep betrayal and I have nothing that I can say that will change any of that."

Alison looked at Brian searchingly. She seemed to see something in him indicating his honesty. She sat back in her chair and said, "You are right. I know that Chad is your friend more than me. I won't speak for him. But, for me, I don't want to see you. I don't want to hear from you. I don't want to even act like you exist."

Brian nodded. "I will leave you alone. But I don't know about Grace. She has questions. You are not really her mother, but for a while she thought you were. She does look like you."

Alison eyes softened and her body sagged. "I just don't think I can handle that right now. It is like having a child you never knew you had. I know she is not mine, but sort of is mine. Tell her not now. It's not a never. But, not now."

Brian agreed. "I think she will accept that. I will send Chad Grace's connect information if she wants you to contact her. That way it is between you two and I'm not involved. I know I said I was sorry, but I do hope you believe me."

Tears started welling in Alison's eyes and her face hardened. "I don't doubt you are, but right now, I can't say as that matters. Please just leave me alone."

With that, Alison disconnected the call.

Chapter Twenty-Nine

SIX MONTHS LATER

Brian sat watching Grace and Alex doing some homework. When it was done, they were going to play video games. This was the third night this week the two had been together. Grace seemed to really be enjoying his company. Brian felt like he was living on borrowed time with his daughter. The last six months had been tumultuous. They had fought often about Alison and all that he had hid from her.

Brian had shared the tech websites with her so that she could come to some understanding of where she came from. He had spent time with her trying to rebuild their relationship. Whenever he looked at her, he could still see that little chubby cheeked, golden haired toddler that used to worship his every move. Peace had come slowly, but they did seem to be working things out.

Chad had started calling. At first, he just called and asked after Grace. But the last time he called, they had talked for almost thirty minutes. Alison and Brian still had not spoken since "that night" as he thought about it. He knew she and Grace had talked a few times. It was awkward for both of them. It was like they both did and did not have a connection.

Chad had told him that he thought Alison might get over things at some point, but he didn't know. Alison had always wanted a daughter, Chad told him. But the betrayal was still hard for her. Brian kept thinking about what he could have done differently. He knew he should have been honest with Chad and Alison immediately, but he also knew that his shame kept him from it. In a way, he was thankful that Grace had discovered Alison. He didn't know if he would have ever told her if not for her discovery.

Brian heard Grace's phone buzz. She called over to her dad, "It's Sandy. I have to take this." As she was headed up the stairs, she called back to Alex, "I will be right back."

Brian felt self-conscious in the silence with Grace leaving. He wandered over to the table and peered over Alex's shoulder at the homework. He noticed that Alex seemed to be dressing better since he started spending time with Grace. His shirt had no holes and his hair smelled freshly washed. Brian even thought he could detect an attempt to style it. "Coding, huh?"

Alex pushed back from the table. "Yup. It always amazes me how great Grace is. She must get that from you."

Brian shrugged his shoulder. He worked with computers for much of the day, but he really didn't code. "She works most of it out herself."

Alex smiled. "I have really liked spending time with her. She's not like other girls."

Brian frowned unsure what Alex meant.

Alex stammered, "She is just so nice. So many of the girls I meet are just so stuck up. You would think it would kill them to talk to you or something."

Brian listened still unsure. He could see that a young man like Alex would find lots of rejection because of the way he dressed and talked, but he feared Alex was meaning something more. Alex did not seem to sense Brian's confusion and kept on.

"So many girls only care about looks and money. If you don't have one or the other, they won't give you the time of day. I used to think that they shouldn't be allowed to pick who they dated, but then I met Grace."

Brian felt himself getting more and more uncomfortable. Alex was starting to sound like some of the men on the message boards. Brian couldn't believe it. He had seemed so nice. "I'm not sure I know what you mean," Brian prompted.

"I just figured you would understand. I mean you aren't married and don't date. I just thought that you would get it," Alex answered.

Brian took a step back. He didn't want to come out and ask Alex if he was an incel, but he was beginning to wonder. Brian decided to try something, "It would be easier if it was one girl one guy. You would know where you stood and wouldn't have to worry about some people having all the fun."

Alex's face lit up. His eyes widened, showing their dark green color, as he smiled. "Exactly. I knew you got it. Where do women get off thinking they can just date whoever they want? Why does some guy get to date like ten women and another guy gets no one? I'm glad to see you raised Grace up right. She doesn't just care about looks like some of her dumb friends."

Brian gripped the back of the chair in front of him until his fingers were turning white trying to get control over his emotions. He couldn't believe that he had never noticed that Alex was an incel. This was horrible. He remembered how he had suggested to Grace that she date him.

"Don't worry, Mr. Jennings," Alex continued on completely unaware of Brian's inner turmoil. "I promise I will take good care of Grace. I know she's a breeder. I will cherish her. Now that I finally have a girl, I will not ever let her go. One guy, one girl, right? And when we get married and have kids, I will raise them up to understand how we need to change the system."

Brian released the chair, shoving it away. He took a deep breath reminding himself that he could not have a screaming match with Grace upstairs. He had put her through enough over the last few months. They were finally back to a better place. But, also, he could not let Alex pull his daughter deeper into this dark world.

Brian's frantic thoughts raced as he was not able to pull them together to figure out a way to handle this. He could feel a knot forming in the pit of his stomach. Looking towards the stairs, all of his instincts screamed at him to protect Grace.

Making an effort, Brian spoke very slowly and quietly. "I need you to get your books and leave."

Alex gave a quick shake of his head as if he had not heard. "What?"

"I need you to leave. You need to be gone before Grace ever comes back down the stairs. You will never see my daughter again."

Alex sat with a frown on his face, his arms crossed over his chest. "I'm not sure that is your decision."

Brian jerked back as if slapped. "My decision? I have the right to say who is in my house."

Alex gave a snide smile. "But you can't keep me away from Grace. She loves me."

Brian reached out as if to hit Alex. But when Alex jutted his chin out as if daring him to, he stopped. He could not get into a fight with this boy.

"You will leave now," Brian demanded.

Alex sat like stone, smirking at Brian. "You think you can make me leave, old man?"

Brian clenched his fist tight. "You will leave my house now. Or I will make you leave. If you ever come back or ever see Grace again, I will do whatever it takes to make it stop." Brian leaned in making his voice deadly. "Whatever it takes."

Alex continued to smile snidely as he got up from the table, slowly packing up his books and papers. He kept glancing up the stairs towards Grace's bedroom. When he could not delay any longer, he shuffled towards the door. As he pulled it open, he looked back at Brian. "This is not the end of this."

Chapter Thirty

BRIAN

Brian slumped into the chair in front of him. He tried to clear away the tension in his neck by rolling his head and rubbing his neck. He took a few deep breaths as he tried to focus so he could calm down. He was going to have to figure out how to tell Grace. He just did not want to deal with this. Not today, not ever.

When Grace came down the stair, Brian was sitting at the table waiting for her. Her eyes darted around, "Where's Alex?"

"I asked him to leave," Brian informed her.

Grace immediately went to the door, to look out for him. "What? Why? I don't understand."

Brian waited for her to walk back to the table. "We were having a discussion while you were upstairs. I'm afraid he said some things that have me quite concerned."

Grace lowered her eyebrows and frowned. "He always says weird things. It's nothing. What did he say this time that was so bad?"

Brian tried to focus on what he wanted to say to her. "It was not just what he said, but why he said it."

"I still don't understand, Daddy," Grace replied.

"Alex belongs to a group of guys that blame women and girls for not being able to date. They think that girls shouldn't have as much control over who they date. They want every guy to have a girl."

Grace's face clouded with confusion. "What are you talking about? What group? What do you mean? How do you know any of this?"

Brian's face reddened as he knew he would have to tell Grace at least some about his online message boards. He looked out the picture window in front of the table gazing at nothing. This was going to be almost as hard as the discussion about Grace's mother.

"I sort of belong to a group like that," he stated, still not making eye contact.

"Dad, what group? You never go anywhere?"

Brian gave a short laugh. "Don't rub it in," he joked, but then turned serious. "That is part of why I belonged to the group. It used to be that Chad and I would hang out. He would get about any girl that he wanted. He had looks and charm. But I never got a girl. That's how I ended up with the club thing."

"Ew, Dad, you promised we would never talk about that," Grace stated, nose wrinkling.

Brian got a small, sad smile, "No, I'm not going to talk about it. I'm just saying that I never really dated. Like never. That's why I gave you some bad advice. I used to get really down on myself and feel like a failure.

"Anyway, one day, I came across a chat room that had all these guys in it. They had never dated, either. They were all talking about how it is the fault of the women -- girls in your case. It was such a relief to talk with other guys who were going through the same things I was going through. To be able to think it might not be me, but just stupid women.

"So over time, we got message boards and would post about our version of a perfect world. One where every man had one woman and every man got to have sex."

"Dad! Ew. Don't say that word," Grace broke in.

"I'm trying to be serious, Grace. This is important," Brian admonished her.

"I know, Dad, but it all sounds so weird. Did anyone ever consider how they were going to make this all happen?"

Brian answered, "That's the worst part. Some of the men advocated violence and force. They would often divide women into categories of breeders that you marry and whores that you just... well you don't want me to say the word.

"One of the ideas was to make sure to raise any children you had to join this world view so that over time, more and more people would have it."

"How are you going to have any children if you never date?" Grace asked.

Brian thought about it. He could not remember that ever being a topic of conversation. Funny how those that were most negative about their chances of having sex and/or ever dating were sure they were going to have children.

"That might have been a flaw in their plan."

Grace cocked an eyebrow at him, "Not their only flaw."

Brian nodded, "No, not their only one. But the problem becomes that somehow somebody must have tried carrying out the plan. While you were upstairs, Alex called you a breeder. He talked about how it should be one guy and one girl. In fact, I am a little worried for your safety as he implied you are his and he will never let you go."

Grace's eyes filled with hurt and pain as Brian told her what Alex said. "You must have misunderstood him," she stated with tears in her voice. "He would never say things like that about me. Never. I just....

"Why did you even have to talk to him? Everything was just fine until you butted in."

Brian looked at the floor unable to meet Grace's tear-filled eyes. "I couldn't ignore what he said about you. You don't understand how dark some of these people are."

"Are? You mean you still believe all this stuff? You still get on there?" Grace snapped.

Brian hung his head even lower. "It's like a habit. When you were little, after you went to bed, I would get on there. Some days, those were the only people outside of work I ever talked to. They just got me in a way that no one else did."

"Yeah, a crazy, we are all going to hell kind of way," Grace challenged him. "How can you judge Alex and say he can't date me, when you are just like him?"

Brian felt his body go stiff. He had continued to read and post messages, but he had always thought he was just slightly better than many of the ones that were the worst. But was Grace right? Was he no better than they were? He never called them out or challenged the more extreme views when they were posted. Sometimes, he even added to them.

"Look, we can have a discussion about me later, but right now we need to discuss you and Alex. Or more importantly discuss how there is not going to be a you and Alex anymore."

Grace's eyes overflowed with tears and they slowly ran down her face. "But I love him."

Brian reached to hug her. His heart breaking at the sight of her tears. Grace pulled back, making him feel even worse. His hands dropped to his side, clenching into fists as he thought about Alex and the hurt he was causing his daughter.

Brian's heart was breaking as he silently watched Grace. Words failed him. He struggled to fight back his own tears not knowing what he should do. He wanted to reach out to Alison knowing this was more a "mom" thing, but he didn't dare. Finally, he broke the silence, "I know you do, but I worry about you continuing to date him."

Grace snuffled and blotted at her eyes with her hand. "You don't even begin to understand. Like you said, you don't date. You don't know what it feels like to have your heart broken."

Brian disagreed with Grace thinking back to when he tried to date Alison, but he knew Grace would not want to hear it. "I can see you are in pain. I wish I could stop it."

Grace blurted out, "Then let me date him. How can you tell me 'no'? It's not fair. He's just like you. You shouldn't be allowed to be my father."

Brian put a hand over his chest feeling as if he had been

stabbed. It was completely different between being her parent and dating her. She was being unfair.

Brian answered her, "That is not fair. That is not fair at all."

"I don't care if it is fair or not. You seem to think it is okay for you to be one of these people and think horrible things about women, but I can't date someone that thinks the same thing?"

"So you want to date someone that thinks he deserves you just because he deserves a girl? You want to date someone that may believe he is entitled to a girl or sex even if he takes it by force. Whatever else I have done wrong, I have never advocated deliberately hurting women. Never."

Grace snapped back, her anger overcoming her sadness, "But you don't know that Alex does, either. You seem to think you are normal, reading those boards and stuff. Maybe he's normal, also. You never even considered that."

Brian sighed. He hated having Grace yell at him, but her anger was better than tears. "He used phrases that are typical of the violent ones. Granted maybe they just write that stuff and they don't really mean it. But I can't take that risk. All I can think about is what if he hurt you."

Grace's face crumbled from anger to tears. "But he would never hurt me."

Brian reached over and brushed the tears away with his fingers. "I wish I knew that for sure. But I don't think that is true. You will find someone else."

Grace huffed as she swung back to anger. "Meet someone else. Yeah, like the last time you gave me dating advice. I don't think you have any right to tell me anything. You just hook up in VR with women that aren't real and talk to other men that are just as much a loser as you are.

"For all you know, the next time I meet someone he will be just like you, also. I'm going to bed!" Grace shouted, her eyes more brown than usual seemed full of fire and her hair whipped around her face as she turned and stomped up the stairs. At the top, she paused to yell down, "I am going to Sandy's this weekend. That is why she called. Her cousin is visiting and she's having friends over after school. Don't even think I'm not going."

Brian didn't argue. He knew that Sandy still did not like Alex. If Grace was going there, Alex would not be around. Besides, he knew better than to pick a fight with her tonight.

Chapter Thirty-One

GRACE

Grace stood by Sandy's locker shifting from foot to foot impatiently waiting. She could not believe she was not here yet. She really needed to talk to her. She had seen Alex earlier and ducked in the bathroom. She did not think he had seen her, but she wanted Sandy around. After she calmed down, she had thought about all the things her dad had said last night. If Alex really was one of these "incel" people, she was beginning to get a little creeped out about it. She had googled it. The whole idea was repulsive to her.

"No Alex this morning," she heard Sandy say behind her.

"Umm, well, no," she stammered.

Sandy snorted, "Trouble in paradise?"

Grace wasn't sure she wanted to have this conversation, but she couldn't lie to her best friend. "I'm taking a break. Maybe forever. He said some really weird things to my dad last night. I just don't know."

Sandy looked incredulous. "Weird things. You are just now noticing how he says weird things. Hello, have you been paying attention?"

Grace shook her head with irritation. "Stop it, Sandy. I know you don't like him, but he was seriously creeping. He called me a breeder to my dad and stuff. It has to do with this strange group of guys that complain because they can't get dates. I was up half the night reading about it."

"He's an incel! I knew it! Why did he ever say something to your dad? That was beyond stupid," Sandy exclaimed.

"What? Wait. What do you know about incels? How am I the only one that doesn't know about this?" Grace questioned her.

Sandy's face closed down and her body stiffened. "Well, you hear things," she tried to deflect. "So what did he say to your dad?"

Grace put out her hand like a stop sign, "No. You are going to have explain some things to me if you want to hear the rest of it."

At that moment the bell rang for class. Sandy gave her a slight smile. "Not right now. Both our stories are going to have to wait. I will talk to you at lunch."

Grace watched her friend walking away. She felt confused and left out. Her friend seemed to know all about something she had just learned about last night. She would be counting the minutes until lunch when they could talk more.

At lunch, Sandy plopped down in the seat next to Grace. Grace smiled at her around her bite of food. She tried to ask her about the incels, but it came out as a mumble. Swallowing quickly, she demanded, "Spill it. Tell me everything you know. I mean it."

Sandy shrugged. "I don't really know that much. I was doing research on it for my psych class a while back. It was about how small groups can be supportive, but the group dynamics can make a fringe group become more and more extreme. I wrote my paper on the incel movement.

"Anyway, I thought about joining some of the female branches. Since you know…. I don't really date much," Sandy blushed with embarrassment, "but some of the stuff I read as I was reading the forums just made my skin crawl. I decided I didn't want any part of it."

Grace looked at her friend with shock. She had trouble believing either her father or Alex were extremist. Now, Sandy was admitting she was almost one. Did everyone in the world worry this much about dating? Maybe it was a good thing her father had never let her date. But then she thought back to some of the things her father had said. "So how did you know Alex was one?"

Sandy tilted her head and stared over Grace's shoulder, she appeared to be thinking. When she made eye contact with Grace, it was clear that she had made a decision. "I'm not sure exactly. It was more a feeling based on how he talked about women. He never even tried to date, until you, but he had all these theories about why 'men like him' couldn't 'get women'. It just was a lot like the nonsense I read about.

"When he started dating you, I thought maybe I was wrong. Or he would quit the group? I wasn't sure. I thought about telling you, but," Sandy shrugged again, "I didn't want to be wrong. So tell me how did you break up?"

"When I was on the phone with you about this weekend, he said some things to my dad. My dad knew about incels because…. Well, because he does," Grace hesitated to tell Sandy about her dad. "Anyway, my dad said that I can't date him."

Grace's eyes slowly filled with tears and her voice quavered, "I don't know what to think. I thought I really liked him, but now, I'm not sure I even know him."

Sandy sighed. "I should have warned you."

"I'm not sure I would have believed you. He even told my dad that he can't keep me from him. That really creeped me out. What if he tries something?"

Sandy chuckled. "All the more reason to come over this weekend. You can meet my cousin, we can have some fun, and Alex won't know where you are."

Grace smiled and nodded. "It sounds perfect. I'm sure Dad will let me come."

Chapter Thirty-Two

BRIAN

Brian sat at his computer horrified. He had not been on the boards in days. Since Grace and him had talked, he had been unsure of if he wanted to keep doing the forums. But with her at Sandy's for the weekend, he decided he wanted to check them out. He had not been prepared for the posts he found.

It appeared that Alex was posting on the boards. Someone named TooLonelyAgain had posted about his attempts to date under the heading INCEL HAS DAUGHTER. The post chronicled how he found an appropriate "breeder" and started dating her. It discussed how the girl's dad had recognized him as an Incel, because he was one also. But then the dad had made him stop seeing her. The replies were brutal. They demanded that the original poster name the father and daughter.

Another member, who appeared to be Alex's father, TooLonely, discussed how he had "raised my son right" and that others needed to step up and do the same for their daughters. Brian's concern turned to fear as he read the posts. Some of the posts were crying for TooLonelyAgain to take revenge. They not only wanted to know who the incel was, but were encouraging Alex to "take her by force."

Some of the group members had been reading the archives. Several posts were title COULD THIS BE HIM? or FOUND HIM. Reading them, Brian could see where they had found something a member had posted that either stated or implied they were a father. He tried to remember if he had ever posted anything that could be used as he was scanning each post to see if he had been outed.

When he finally had enough, Brian pushed back from the desk, putting his head in his hands. He could feel a headache building. He didn't know what to do to protect Grace. He realized that Alex knew where he lived. All he would have to do was post Grace's name, address, and photo. Brian felt tears dripping off the end of his nose as he contemplated the danger he had placed his daughter in. He debated with himself what to do.

An alert told him he had received an email. Brian pulled it up.

Have you seen the message boards? You really should give her up to me. Make this easier on yourself and on her. Just remember, I can out you at any time.

   Alex

Brian twisted around looking at the windows behind him. He felt eyes on him, even though he knew no one was there. It was as if Alex had known he was on the boards. A chill went down Brian's spine, even as he told himself that was ridiculous.

Brian jumped as his computer chimed telling him he had an incoming call. He almost panicked until he realized it was from Grace. Sweat dripped down his back as he accepted the call.

"Dad! Dad! Guess what? You will never guess what happened," Grace exclaimed.

Brian felt his fear rise as numerous ominous situations went through his head. But then he realized that Grace was excited. Shakily, he answered, "No, I probably will never guess. Why don't you just tell me."

Grace reached beside her and pulled a young man in the picture. He appeared to be her age, or slightly younger. He looked like he could have just stepped off a fashion magazine. He had that, "I just got out of bed look" that Brian could remember Chad having back in the day. Brian had never understood how looking so causal could look so put together at the same time.

"This is Sam, Sandy's cousin," Grace announced. "We are coming over to see you. You just have to meet him. He is great. I think you will really like him."

Grace babbled on as Brian made eye contact with Sam. The perfect hair, perfect clothes, perfect smile. Brian doubted this young man ever lacked for a date. When his brain finally caught up to what Grace was saying, he groaned inside. "No, no, no," he thought, "why would she have to find a boy like this."

Brian took in Grace's smile and her flushed cheeks. Her eyes were burning with an intensity he had not seen all week, since her and Alex had broken up. Grace must have sensed something was wrong. She pulled away from Sam and said, "Let me talk to him for a minute."

As she moved away, Grace lowered her voice, "It's okay, Dad. I know he's not an incel. He's dated other girls and Sandy says he's great. I really like him. Can we please come over?"

Brian mentally shook his head. Oh to be a teenager and so resilient again. It was just days ago that Grace was broken-hearted. But he really couldn't deny her at least meeting this boy. After the last few days, he felt he owed her at least that. "Okay. Come on over."

Brian watched as Grace's smile grew even bigger and she laughed. "You will like him. I know you will."

As Brian ended the call, he returned to the email and the message board. He knew if Alex figured out that Grace had moved on, that would only make him bolder. But what could he do, call the police and tell them what?

This guy that wants to date my daughter is crazy and I know because I belong to the same crazy group?

Brian rubbed his face thinking. The only thing he could think to do was to confront Alex head on and not show the fear he was feeling. Pulling up the email, he replied.

Alex

I would hope that you would not post any personal information about me or my daughter on the forum. To do so would be a violation of several privacy laws. At this point, Grace and I want nothing more to do with you. Please do not contact either of us again or this will be a matter for the police.

Brian

Brian sent the email then returned to the boards. He checked for any new posts, but it seemed calm right now. He figured it was just a matter of time until Alex posted something or an old post of his would be brought to light. Knowing he could do nothing to prevent either, Brian shut down his system and went to get ready for Grace and her guest.

Chapter Thirty-Three

BRIAN

Brian was just sitting brownies on the table when he heard Grace coming in the front door with Sam in tow. "I have brownies," he called.

Grace hustled into the room, her hair appearing coppery in the afternoon sun, swirled around her face. Sam walked behind her -- appearing even more handsome in person. He reminded Brian of what he could have looked like if he would have been thinner and more fashionable when he was younger. Sam's hair was so dark brown, it appeared almost black. His eyes were dark brown. He had a firm chin and high cheekbones, making his face appear as if it had been sculpted for a Greek god.

"Nice to meet you, Mr. Jennings." Sam walked forward with his hand out to shake Brian's hand. Brian found himself charmed by the young man in spite of himself. He reached out and shook his hand, gesturing towards the table afterwards. "Let me get you both something to drink."

Brian watched as Sam pulled out Grace's chair, then leaned down and whispered in her ear. Grace giggled and pushed him away. Sam straightened and looked at Brian. "It is nice to meet you. Grace has told me so much about you."

When Brian returned from getting everyone some iced tea, he found Sam dishing up some brownies for Grace. He had turned one of the chairs around backwards, sitting straddle on it. Smiling at Grace, Brain could tell Sam had just made her laugh again.

"Grace, here is the iced tea," Brian stated.

Grace started to jump up, when Sam put his hand on her arm. "Let me."

Brian wasn't sure if Sam was trying to impress him, Grace, or was just naturally polite, but he seemed to be much more interested in Grace's feelings than Alex ever was. Brian smiled inside. It was nice to see Grace happy again.

As they ate, Grace told her dad about Sam and how he was visiting Sandy, but his family might move here. She seemed quite enthralled with him. The more Sam talked, Brian began to detect a slight Southern accent.

"Where are you from?" Brian asked him.

"My dad is in the Navy. I was born and lived my early life in North and South Carolina. Since then we have moved around quite a bit. Now that he's out, I'm hoping that we get to stay in one place for a while."

"I thought I heard an accent," Brian declared.

Sam blushed, "Yes, sir. I used to have more of one, but all the moving has made me lose most of it. It does come back when I'm real angry or I'm tired."

Brian and Sam talked about what it was like to move around during childhood as Grace listened. Brian felt like Sam was putting in an effort to make Brian like him, but he also believed that Sam was naturally charming and polite. Brian really didn't want to like him, but he could not find one reason not to.

Brian caught Grace glancing at him on a few occasions. He knew she was trying to gauge his reaction to Sam. After the last of the brownies were gone, he excused himself to take the plates back to the kitchen. Standing in front of the sink, Brian leaned against the counter. He drew in his breaths in deep pulls. He really didn't know what to do.

This boy - Sam - seemed nice enough, but just from the time Brian had spent with him, he knew this boy was going to be one of those young men that could have any girl they wanted. Brian knew that should not bother him because right now he wanted Grace. But he also knew this young man would think much of what Brian had believed his whole life was a joke. He would no more understand what it meant to be an incel than Chad did.

But was understanding that great? Brian asked himself. Look at Alex. He understood it and now Brian was scared of what he might do to Grace.

"Daddy," Brian heard. Turning, he saw Grace standing just inside the kitchen door.

"You were taking so long I thought something had happened," she commented.

Brian looked at her. He tried to see things from her view. Sam was smart, attractive, and charming. He seemed attentive to her and as if he wanted her to be happy. Who knew if or when he would move on to another girl, but right now Grace was happy.

"I was just thinking," he answered her.

"About Sam?"

Brian nodded. "Yes. You really seem to like him."

Grace wiggled her hand back and forth in front of her. "I don't really know him, but he's fun. I like spending time with him."

Brian smiled at her. "I think that is probably the most important thing."

Grace smiled. "Really?"

"Yes. He is not what I would have had in mind if I would have designed a boyfriend for you. But you are happy. He's nice. And I'm fresh out of computer programmed boyfriends."

Grace twirled, rushing out of the kitchen laughing. "Sam, you want to head out to the movies?"

Brian followed slowly. When he got to the front room, Grace and Sam were ready to leave. But Sam walked over and shook his hand again. "I will have her home on time tonight. She is safe with me, sir."

With that they headed out. Brian watched from the window until they had driven out of sight. He still wasn't sure if this was a good idea or not. But ultimately Grace was going to have to find the right guy for her. It was not up to him.

Chapter Thirty-Four

BRIAN

Brian decided it was time to face the message boards. He was going to have to come to some decision about what to do with his forum. He dreaded logging back on. But he knew he had to check to see if anything had happened while he was offline. When he got online, Brian found that it was worst then he expected.

TIMETODATE had posted that he had "discovered" who the incel was. Brian did not remember this member and wondered if Alex had created a false account. Even with his admin privileges, he was not always able to detect who really owned an account. This member had flagged a post Brian had made years ago about how he just didn't know if he was capable of raising a daughter.

Our own admin has a child. A girl child. Even if this is not the person TooLonelyAgain was referring to he owes us.

Brian looked at the post and the replies coming almost faster than he could read them.

"How does he think he rates? He needs to share with the rest of us," wrote one poster.

This was followed by calls on Brian to "share her" and various scenarios were given. The original poster had suggested a lottery.

We can all put our names in. Whoever has their name drawn gets her.

Brian read the post feeling his horror turn to anger. Grace was a sixteen-year-old girl. These men were talking about her as if she were just a thing to possess. How dare they act as if they had a right to her, just because she had an incel for a father. How did that make her any different from any other girl?

Brian posted, "She is my daughter. I am not going to just randomly draw some guy's name out of a hat, she's not even an adult."

The response was instant. Members began calling him names and taunting him. Someone pulled up his creed from right before he had Grace. Other members challenged him to auction her. Brian felt his anger building.

"You are all despicable," he wrote. "She is still a child. Why would I auction her off like livestock? She deserves better. You have no right to tell me how to raise my daughter or who she can date. I used to think coming on here saved my sanity.

"You all understood what it was like to be lonely. To want a companion. To know how it felt to believe you would be alone the rest of your life. But now you are hate filled and it is no wonder no one wants to date any of you.

"I will not be giving my daughter away in a drawing or auctioning her off. In fact, if I can prevent it, I will never have her date any of you. EVER."

Brian felt trepidation and freedom as he pushed send. He knew this could result in more problems with his forum. But he could not let them threaten Grace. Maybe she was right. If he was going to be part of this, it was as if he was giving approval for the things they posted.

Brian was not surprised to see an almost instant response. Sadly, he was not even that surprised at what they said. Some of the members called for him to be banned from the group. Others called for anyone that knew where he lived to out him. Brian knew it was only a matter of time before Alex or someone else did it. He would not be able to protect Grace at that point.

The group members might all be keyboard cowboys, but he couldn't risk that. Brian called up a program that he had written when he created the forum. If he hit execute, it would work its way through the INCEL forum like a worm virus destroying everything. When it was done, it would be as if the site had never existed. Even cache version of postings would be gone.

Brian's finger hovered over the execute key. He knew that if he did this, he would be saying goodbye to everyone. All of his "friends". All of the postings. Everything. But as he sat there. He realized if the choice was between this group and Grace, there really was no choice. She was his daughter.

With tears spilling down his face, Brian hit execute and turned his back on the incel world he had created.

Chapter Thirty-Five

SIX MONTHS LATER

Brian watched as Grace and Sam left on another date. Since Sam had moved to town, they went out at least once a week. Sam continued to seem very polite and caring. Brian heard an incoming alert. Turning, he saw Chad was screening him.

"Yes," he answered. Then blinked in surprise. It was Chad and Alison on the screen.

"Hello," he stammered.

Alison smiled slightly. "Hi Brian. Chad and I…. Well, mostly it was me, but I made Chad join me for moral support," Alison stated. "We wanted to let you know that you have raised a wonderful girl. I talk to Grace at least once a week. Sometimes more. I know it must have been hard for you to let her and I talk without you knowing anything about it," Alison continued.

Brian nodded in agreement. "It was the least I could do. I owed you so much."

Alison stated, "I wanted to thank you for leaving me alone. It gave me time to think. You know I was not really very nice to you myself. I knew you wanted to date me, and I used that to get to Chad. I was mean and unfair to you."

"It was so long ago," Brian interjected.

"As was what you did. I will admit, it does still bother me at times. I will catch Grace making a movement and it is so much like me, it takes my breath away. Then I remember how she was created. But that was in the past.

"The reason I'm calling now is because I think it is time to put the past in the past. We, Chad and I, would like to have you and Grace over for supper sometime soon."

Brian felt his eyes prickle with tears. "I don't deserve this. What I did was so wrong."

Alison answered, "But had you not done it, we all would not have Grace and she is truly a wonder. However, she was created you have raised her well. Please come to dinner soon."

With that, Alison left the screen. Brian looked at Chad, questions on his face. Chad smiled. "She means it. Her and Grace had a long talk about two weeks ago. Grace told her everything. About the incels, the forums, Alex, and this new boy, Sam. I'm not even sure of everything they talked about.

"But after that, she kept saying how we had not been fair to you. I think the idea of you having sex with her without her really being involved still bothers her. But she is really trying to put it behind her. Come to dinner."

With that Chad signed off. Brian -- out habit that he still had not completely broken -- reached for his keyboard to log into the INCEL forum. Then he remembered how he had "killed it".

There were days that he regretted that. He still thought about joining another message board or starting a new forum of his own. But he knew that he couldn't. Every time he started to reach out, he thought of the things they had said about Grace. Over the last few months, he was slowly learning to live without the group. In fact, as he reached for his VR suit, he had plans tonight and now he was running late.

Brian carefully put on his VR suit. He loaded up his programs. After making sure everything was running, he entered his destination. Brian found himself outside a club. It was more of the quieter ones that catered to an "older" crowd. He figured that applied to him now. The bouncer scanned him with a wand and produced a blue bracelet. Brian smiled. He had used some slight mods, but had kept it under the 25% threshold.

The bouncer handed Brian a list of rules and options to check. Brian closely read through the paperwork. When he was done, he went back and made sure he had checked 'NO' for the pregnancy option. Paperwork complete, the bouncer waved him into the club.

Afterword

www.MR-Richardson.com

If you like this book, please leave a review. The only way I can decide whether to commit more time to these characters and this series is by getting feedback from you, the readers. Your opinion matters to me. I have only so much time to craft new stories. Help me invest that time wisely.

If you enjoyed this story check out others by the Shadow Kai Writing group

If you like to check out my other works click one of the following links

Galactic Mandate: A Radical Cause
   Galactic Mandate: The Scream
   NO MORE SUPERHUMANS: FREEDOM OR DEATH